W. H. G. Kingston

Stories of Animal Sagacity

W. H. G. Kingston

Stories of Animal Sagacity

ISBN/EAN: 9783744750547

Printed in Europe, USA, Canada, Australia, Japan

Cover: Foto ©Andreas Hilbeck / pixelio.de

More available books at **www.hansebooks.com**

STORIES

OF

ANIMAL SAGACITY.

BY

W. H. G. KINGSTON,

AUTHOR OF "IN THE EASTERN SEAS," "IN THE WILDS OF AFRICA," "ON THE
BANKS OF THE AMAZON," ETC.

With Sixty Illustrations by Harrison Weir

LONDON:
T. NELSON AND SONS, PATERNOSTER ROW;
EDINBURGH; AND NEW YORK.
1875.

CONTENTS.

CHAPTER I.
Cats.

CHAPTER II.
Dogs.

CHAPTER III.

Horses.

CHAPTER IV.

Donkeys.

CHAPTER V.

Elephants.

CHAPTER VI.

Oxen.

CHAPTER VII.

Savage and Other Animals.

CHAPTER VIII.

Birds.

CHAPTER I.

Cats.

HAVE undertaken, my young friends, to give you a number of anecdotes, which will, I think, prove that animals possess not only instinct, which guides them in obtaining food, and enables them to enjoy their existence according to their several natures, but also that many of them are capable of exercising a kind of reason, which comes into play under circumstances to which they are not naturally exposed.

Those animals more peculiarly fitted to be the companions of man, and to assist him in his occupations, appear to possess generally a larger amount of this power; at all events, we have better opportunities of noticing it, although, probably, it exists also in a certain degree among wild animals.

I will commence with some anecdotes of the sagacity shown by animals with which you are all well acquainted —Cats and Dogs; and if you have been accustomed to watch the proceedings of your dumb companions you will be able to say, "Why, that is just like what Tabby once did ; " or, " Our Ponto acted nearly as cleverly as that the other day."

<hr />

THE CAT AND THE KNOCKER.

WHEN you see Pussy seated by the fireside, blinking her eyes, and looking very wise, you may often ask, " I wonder what she can be thinking about." Just then, probably, she is thinking about nothing at all ; but if you were to turn her out of doors into the cold, and shut the door in her face, she would instantly begin to think, " How can I best get in again ? " And she would run round and round the house, trying to find a door or window open by which she might re-enter it.

I once heard of a cat which exerted a considerable amount of reason under these very circumstances. I am not quite certain of this Pussy's name, but it may possibly have been Deborah. The house where Deborah was born and bred is situated in the country, and there is a door with a small porch opening on a flower-garden. Very often when this door was shut, Deborah, or little Deb, as she may have been called, was left outside ; and on such occasions she used to mew as loudly as she could to beg for admittance. Occasionally she was not heard ; but instead of running away, and trying to find some other home, she used—wise little creature that she was !—patiently to ensconce herself in a corner of the window-sill, and wait till some person came to the house, who, on knocking at the door, found immediate attention. Many a day, no doubt, little Deb sat there on the window-sill and watched this proceeding, gazing at the

THE CAT AND THE KNOCKER.

knocker, and wondering what it had to do with getting the door open.

A month passed away, and little Deb grew from a kitten into a full-sized cat. Many a weary hour was passed in her corner. At length Deb arrived at the conclusion that if she could manage to make the knocker sound a rap-a-tap-tap on the door, the noise would summon the servant, and she would gain admittance as well as the guests who came to the house.

One day Deb had been shut out, when Mary, the maid-servant, who was sitting industriously stitching away, heard a rap-a-tap at the front door, announcing the arrival, as she supposed, of a visitor. Putting down her work, she hurried to the door and lifted the latch; but no one was there except Deb, who at that moment leaped off the window-sill and entered the house. Mary looked along the road, up and down on either side, thinking that some person must have knocked and gone away; but no one was in sight.

The following day the same thing happened, but it occurred several times before any one suspected that Deb could possibly have lifted the knocker. At length Mary told her mistress what she suspected, and one of the family hid in the shrubbery to watch Deb's proceedings. Deb was allowed to run out in the garden, and the door was closed. After a time the little creature was seen to climb up on the window-sill, and then to rear herself on her hind-feet, in an oblique position at the full stretch of her body, when, steadying herself with one front paw, with the other she raised the knocker; and Mary, who was on the watch, instantly ran to the door and let her in.

Miss Deb's knock now became as well known to the servant as that of any other member of the family, and, no doubt to her great satisfaction, it usually met with prompt attention.

Could the celebrated cat of the renowned Marquis of Carrabas have done more, or better? Not only must Deb have exercised reason and reflection, as well as imitation, but a considerable amount of perseverance; for probably she made many vain attempts before she was rewarded with success.

Some Scotch ladies told me of a cat they had when young, brought by their grandfather from Archangel, which, under the same circumstances, used to reach up to the latch of the front door of a house in the country, and to rattle away on it till admitted. I have seen a cat which the same ladies now possess make a similar attempt.

Does it not occur to you that you may take a useful lesson from little Pussy, and when you have an object to gain, a task to perform, think over the matter, and exert yourself to the utmost till you have accomplished it?

THE CAT AND THE RABBIT-TRAP.

AN instance of the sagacity of a cat came under my own notice. I was living, a few years ago, in a country place in Dorsetshire, when one day a small tortoise-shell cat met my children on the road, and followed them home. They, of course, petted and stroked her, and showed their wish to make her their friend. She was one of the smallest,

and yet the most active of full-grown cats I ever saw.
From the first she gave evidence of being of a wild and
predatory disposition, and made sad havoc among the
rabbits, squirrels, and birds. I have several times seen
her carry along a rabbit half as big as herself. Many
would exclaim that for so nefarious a deed she ought to
have been shot; but as she had tasted of my salt, taken
refuge under my roof, besides being the pet of my children,
I could not bring myself to order her destruction.

We had, about the time of her arrival, obtained a dog
to act as a watchman over the premises. She and he were
at first on fair terms—a sort of armed neutrality. In process of time, however, she became the mother of a litter of
kittens. With the exception of one, they shared the fate
of other kittens. When she discovered the loss of her
hopeful family, she wandered about in a melancholy way,
evidently searching for them, till, encountering Carlo, it
seemed suddenly to strike her that he had been the cause
of her loss. With back up, she approached, and flying at
him with the greatest fury, attacked him till blood dropped
from his nose, when, though ten times her size, he fairly
turned tail and fled. Pussy and Carlo, after this, became
friends; at least, they never interfered with each other.

Pussy, however, to her cost, still continued her hunting
expeditions. The rabbits had committed great depredations
in the garden, and the gardener had procured two rabbit-
traps. One had been set at a considerable distance from the
house, and fixed securely in the ground. One morning the
nurse heard a plaintive mewing at the window of the day-
nursery on the ground-floor. She opened it, and in crawled

poor Pussy, dragging the heavy iron rabbit-trap, in the teeth of which her fore-foot was caught. I was called in, and assisted to release her. Her paw swelled, and for some time she could not move out of the basket in which she was placed before the fire. Though suffering intense pain, she must have perceived that the only way to release herself was to dig up the trap, and then drag it, up many steep paths, to the room where her kindest friends—nurse and the children—were to be found.

Carlo had been caught before in the same trap, and he bit at it, and at everything around, and severely injured the gardener, who went to release him. Thus Pussy, under precisely the same circumstances, showed by far the greatest amount of sagacity and cool courage. She, however, not many weeks after her recovery, came in one day with her foot sadly lacerated, having again been caught in a trap; so, although she could reason, she did not appear to have learned wisdom from experience. This last misfortune, however, taught her prudence, as she was never again caught in a trap.

You will agree with me that Pussy was wise in going to her best friends for help when in distress; and foolish, having once suffered, again to run into the same danger.

You, my young reader, will be often entrapped, if you lack strength to resist temptation. Your kind friends at home will, I am sure, help you as far as they have the power; but, that they may do so, you must on all occasions trust them.

AFFECTION EXHIBITED BY A CAT.

I WAS one day calling in Dorsetshire on a clever, kind old
lady, who showed me a beautiful tabby cat, coiled up before
the fire. "Seventeen years ago," said she, "that cat's
mother had a litter. They were all ordered to be drowned
with the exception of one. The servant brought me one.
It was a tortoise-shell. 'No,' I said; 'that will always be
looking dirty. I will choose another.' So I put my hand
into the basket, and drew forth this tabby. The tabby has
loved me ever since. When she came to have a family, she
disappeared; but the rain did not, for it came pouring down
through the ceiling: and it was discovered that Dame Tabby
had made a lying-in hospital for herself in the thatched roof
of the house. The damage she did cost several pounds; so
we asked a friend who had a good cook, fond of cats, to
take care of Tabby the next time she gave signs of having a
family, as we knew she would be well fed. We sent her
in a basket completely covered up; and she was shut into a
room, where she soon exhibited a progeny of young mewlings. More than the usual number were allowed to sur-
vive, and it was thought that she would remain quietly
where she was. Not so. On the first opportunity she
made her escape, and down she came all the length of the
village, and early in the morning I heard her mewing at
my bed-room door to be let in. When I had stroked her
back and spoken kindly to her, off she went to look after
her nurslings. From that day, every morning she came
regularly to see me, and would not go away till she had

been spoken to and caressed. Having satisfied herself that I was alive and well, back she would go. She never failed to pay me that one visit in the morning, and never came twice in the day, till she had weaned her kittens; and that very day she came back, and nothing would induce her to go away again. I had not the heart to force her back. From that day to this she has always slept at the door of my room."

Surely you will not be less grateful to those who brought you up than was my old friend's cat to her. Acts, not mere words, show the sincerity of our feelings. Consider how you are acting towards them each hour and day of your life. Are you doing your best to act well, whether at home, at school, or at play?

THE CAT AND HER YOUNG MISTRESSES.

My friend Mrs. F—— gave me a very touching anecdote. A lady she knew, residing in Essex, once had two young daughters. They had a pet cat which they had reared from a kitten, and which was their constant companion. The sisters, however, were both seized with scarlet fever, and died. The cat seemed perfectly to understand what had taken place, and, refusing to leave the room, seated herself on the bed where they lay, in most evident sorrow. When the bodies of the young girls were placed in their small coffins, she continued to move backwards and forwards from one to the other, uttering low and melancholy sounds. Nothing could induce her all the time to take food, and soon after the interment of her fond playmates she lay down and passed away from life.

This account, given by the mother of the children, makes me quite ready to believe in the truth of similar anecdotes.

Tender affection is like a beautiful flower : it needs cultivation. As cold winds and pelting showers injure the fair blossoms, so passionate temper, sullen behaviour, or misconduct, will destroy the love which should exist between brothers and sisters, and those whose lot is cast together. Cherish affectionate feelings in your hearts. Be kind and gentle to all around, and your friends will love you more even than the cat I have told you about loved her mistresses.

THE CAT WHICH DIED OF GRIEF.

A LADY in France possessed a cat which exhibited great affection for her. She accompanied her everywhere, and when she sat down always lay at her feet. From no other hands than those of her mistress would she take food, nor would she allow any one else to fondle her.

The lady kept a number of tame birds; but the cat, though she would willingly have caught and eaten strange birds, never injured one of them.

At last the lady fell ill, when nothing could induce the cat to leave her chamber ; and on her death, the attendants had to carry away the poor animal by force. The next morning, however, she was found in the room of death.

THE CAT WHICH DIED OF GRIEF.

creeping slowly about, and mewing piteously.   After the
funeral, the faithful cat made her escape from the house,
and was at length discovered stretched out lifeless above
the grave of her mistress, having evidently died of a broken
heart.

The instances I have given—and I might give many
more—prove the strong affection of which cats are capable,
and show that they are well deserving of kind treatment.
When we see them catch birds and mice, we must remember that it is their nature to do so, as in their wild state
they have no other means of obtaining food.

THE CAT AND THE CANARY.

ANIMALS of a very different character often form curious
friendships.   What do you think of the cat which of her
own accord became the protector of a pet canary, instead of
eating it up?

The cat and the bird belonged to the mother-in-law of
Mrs. Lee, who has given us many delightful anecdotes of
animals.   The canary was allowed to fly about the room
when the cat was shut out; but one day their mistress,
lifting her head from her work, saw that the cat had by
some means got in; and, to her amazement, there was the
canary perched fearlessly on the back of Pussy, who seemed
highly pleased with the confidence placed in her.   By the
silent language with which animals communicate their ideas
to each other, she had been able to make the canary understand that she would not hurt it.

After this, the two were allowed to be constantly together, to their mutual satisfaction. One morning, however, as they were in the bed-room of their mistress, what was her dismay to see the trustworthy cat, as she had supposed her, after uttering a feline growl, seize the canary in her mouth, and leap with her into the bed. There she stood, her tail stiffened out, her hair bristling, and her eyes glaring fiercely. The fate of the poor canary appeared sealed; but just then the lady caught sight of a strange cat creeping cautiously through the open doorway. The intruder was quickly driven away, when faithful Puss deposited her feathered friend on the bed, in no way injured—she having thus seized it to save it from the fangs of the stranger.

Confidence begets confidence; but be very sure that the person on whom you bestow yours is worthy of it. If not, you will not be as fortunate as the canary was with its feline friend.

Your truest confidants, in most cases, are your own parents.

THE CAT AND THE FROG.

I HAVE an instance of a still stranger friendship to mention. The servants of a country-house—and I am sure that they were kind people—had enticed a frog from its hole by giving it food. As winter drew on, Froggy every evening made its way to the kitchen hearth before a blazing fire, which it found much more comfortable than its own dark abode out in the yard. Another occupant of the hearth was a favourite old cat, which at first, I daresay, looked down on the odd little creature with some contempt, but was too well bred to disturb an invited guest. At length, however, the two came to a mutual understanding; the kind heart of Pussy warming towards poor chilly little Froggy, whom she now invited to come and nestle under her cozy fur. From that time forward, as soon as Froggy came out of its hole, it hopped fearlessly towards the old cat, who constituted herself its protector, and would allow no one to disturb it.

Imitate the kind cat, and be kind to the most humble, however odd their looks. Sometimes at school and elsewhere you may find some friendless little fellow. Prove his protector. Be not less benevolent than a cat.

THE CAT AND HER DEAD KITTEN.

THAT cats expect those to whom they are attached to sympathize with them in their sorrow, is shown by an affecting story told by Dr. Good, the author of the "Book of Nature."

He had a cat which used to sit at his elbow hour after hour while he was writing, watching his hand moving over the paper. At length Pussy had a kitten to take care of, when she became less constant in her attendance on her master. One morning, however, she entered the room, and leaping on the table, began to rub her furry side against his hand and pen, to attract his attention. He, supposing that she wished to be let out, opened the door; but instead

THE CAT AND THE FROG.

of running forward, she turned round and looked earnestly at him, as though she had something to communicate. Being very busy, he shut the door upon her, and resumed his writing. In less than an hour, the door having been opened again, he felt her rubbing against his feet; when, on looking down, he saw that she had placed close to them the dead body of her kitten, which had been accidentally killed, and which she had brought evidently that her kind master might mourn with her at her loss. She seemed satisfied when she saw him with the dead kitten in his hand, making inquiries as to how it had been killed; and when it was buried, believing that her master shared her sorrow, she gradually took comfort, and resumed her station at his side.

Observe how, in her sorrow, Pussy went to her best friend for sympathy. Your best earthly friends are your parents. Do not hesitate to tell them your griefs; and you will realize that it is their joy and comfort to sympathize with you in all your troubles, little or great, and to try to relieve them.

THE KITTEN AND THE CHICKENS.

KITTENS, especially if deprived of their natural protectors, seem to long for the friendship of other beings, and will often roam about till they find a person in whom they think they may confide. Sometimes they make a curious choice.

A kitten born on the roof of an out-house was by an accident deprived of its mother and brethren. It evaded all attempts to catch it, though food was put within its reach.

Just below where it lived, a brood of chickens were constantly running about; and at length, growing weary of solitude, it thought that it would like to have such lively little playmates. So down it scrambled, and timidly crept towards them. Finding that they were not likely to do it harm, it lay down among them. The chickens seemed to know that it was too young to hurt them.

It now followed them wherever they moved to pick up their food. In a short time a perfect understanding was established between the kitten and the fowls, who appeared especially proud of their new friend. The kitten, discovering this, assumed the post of leader, and used to conduct them about the grounds, amusing itself at their expense. Sometimes it would catch hold of their feet, as if going to bite them, when they would peck at it in return. At others it would hide behind a bush, and then springing out into their midst, purr and rub itself against their sides. One pullet was its especial favourite; it accompanied her every day to her nest under the boards of an out-house, and would then lie down outside, as if to watch over her. When she returned to the other fowls, it would follow, setting up its tail, and purring at her.

When other chickens were born, it transferred its interest to them, taking each fresh brood under its protection—the parent hen appearing in no way alarmed at having so unusual a nurse for her young ones.

Be as sensible as the little kitten. Don't stand on your dignity, or keep upon the roof, in a fit of the sulks; but jump down, and shake such feelings off with a game of good-natured play.

THE CAT AND THE PIGEON.

SIMILAR affection for one of the feathered race was shown by a cat which was rearing several kittens.

In another part of the loft a pigeon had built her nest; but her eggs and young having been frequently destroyed by rats, it seemed to occur to her that she should be in safer quarters near the cat. Pussy, pleased with the confidence placed in her, invited the pigeon to remain near her, and a strong friendship was established between the two. They fed out of the same dish; and when Pussy was absent, the pigeon, in return for the protection afforded her against the rats, constituted herself the defender of the kittens—and on any person approaching nearer than she liked, she would fly out and attack them with beak and wings, in the hope of driving them away from her young charges. Frequently, too, after this, when neither the kittens nor her own brood required her care, and the cat went out about the garden or fields, the pigeon might be seen fluttering close by her, for the sake of her society.

Help and protect one another in all right things, as did the cat and the pigeon, whatever your respective ages or stations in life. The big boy or girl may be able to assist and protect the little ones, who may render many a service in return.

THE CAT AND THE PIGEON.

THE CAT AND THE LEVERET.

CATS exhibit their affectionate nature in a variety of ways. If deprived of their kittens, they have a yearning for the care of some other young creatures, which they will gratify when possible.

A cat had been cruelly deprived of all her kittens. She was seen going about mewing disconsolately for her young ones. Her owner received about the same time a leveret, which he hoped to tame by feeding it with a spoon. One morning, however, the leveret was missing, and as it could nowhere be discovered, it was supposed to have been carried off and killed by some strange cat or dog. A fortnight had elapsed, when, as the gentleman was seated in his garden, in the dusk of the evening, he observed his cat, with tail erect, trotting towards him, purring and calling in the way cats do to their kittens. Behind her came, gambolling merrily, and with perfect confidence, a little leveret,—the very one, it was now seen, which had disappeared. Pussy, deprived of her kittens, had carried it off and brought it up instead, bestowing on it the affection of her maternal heart.

It is your blessed privilege to have hearts to feel the greatest enjoyment in tender love for others. See that you keep that love in constant exercise, or, like others of our best gifts, it may grow dull by disuse or abuse. The time may come when, deprived of your parents or brothers and sisters, you will bitterly mourn the sorrow you have caused by your evil temper or neglect.

THE CAT AND THE PUPPIES.

I HAVE a longer story than the last to tell, of a cat which undertook the nursing of some puppies while she already had some kittens of her own. It happened that her mistress possessed a valuable little black spaniel, which had a litter of five puppies. As these were too many for the spaniel to bring up, and the mistress was anxious to have them all preserved, it was proposed that they should be brought up by hand. The cook, to whom the proposal was made, suggested that this would be a difficult undertaking; but as the cat had lately kittened, some of the puppies might be given to her to bring up. Two of the kittens were accordingly taken away, and the same number of puppies substituted. What Puss thought of the matter has not transpired, or whether even she discovered the trick that had been played her; but be that as it may, she immediately began to bestow the same care on the little changelings that she had done on her own offspring, and in a fortnight they were as forward and playful as kittens would have been, gambolling about, and barking lustily—while the three puppies nursed by their own mother were whining and rolling about in the most helpless fashion.

Puss had proved a better nurse than the little spaniel. She gave them her tail to play with, and kept them always in motion and amused, so that they ate meat, and were strong enough to be removed and to take care of themselves, long before their brothers and sisters.

On their being taken away from her, their poor nurse

showed her sorrow, and went prowling about the house, looking for them in every direction. At length she caught sight of the spaniel and the three remaining puppies. Instantly up went her back; her bristles stood erect, and her eyes glared fiercely at the little dog, which she supposed had carried off her young charges.

" Ho, ho! you vile thief, who have ventured to rob me of my young ones; I have found you at last!" she exclaimed—at least, she thought as much, if she did not say it. The spaniel barked defiance, answering—" They are my own puppies; you know they are as unlike as possible to your little, tiresome, frisky mewlings." "I tell you I know them to be mine," cried Puss, spitting and hissing; "I mean to recover my own." And before the spaniel knew what was going to happen, Puss sprang forward, seized one of the puppies, and carried it off to her own bed in another part of the premises.

Not content with this success, as soon as she had safely deposited the puppy in her home, she returned to the abode of the spaniel. This time she simply dashed forward, as if she had made up her mind what to do, knocked over the spaniel with her paw, seized another puppy in her mouth, and carrying it off, placed it alongside the first she had captured. She was now content. Two puppies she had lost, two she had obtained. Whether or not she thought them the same which had been taken from her, it is difficult to say. At all events, she nursed the two latter with the same tender care as the first.

Copy playful Pussy, when you have charge of little children. They enjoy games of romps as much as young

THE CAT AND THE PUPPIES.

puppies do, and will be far happier, and thrive better, than when compelled to loll about by themselves, while you sit at your book or work in silent dignity and indifference to their requirements, however fond you may be of them—as was, I daresay, the mother spaniel of her pups.

THE CAT AND THE BURGLARS.

No stronger evidence of the sagacity of the cat is to be found than an instance narrated to me by my friend, Mrs. F——, and for which I can vouch.

A lady, Miss P——, who was a governess in her family, had previously held the same position in that of Lord ——, in Ireland. While there a cat became very strongly attached to her. Though allowed to enter the school-room and dining-room, where she was fed and petted, the animal never came into the lady's bed-room; nor was she, indeed, accustomed to go into that part of the house at any time.

One night, however, after retiring to rest, Miss P—— was disturbed by the gentle but incessant mewing of the cat at her bed-room door. At first she was not inclined to pay attention to the cat's behaviour, but the perseverance of the animal, and a peculiarity in the tones of her voice, at length induced her to open the door. The cat, on this, bounded forward, and circled round her rapidly, looking up in her face, mewing expressively. Miss P——, thinking that the cat had only taken a fancy to pay her a visit, refastened the door, intending to let her remain in the room; but this did not appear to please Pussy at all. She sprang back to the door, mewing more loudly than before; then she came again to the lady, and then went to the door, as if asking her to follow.

"What is it you want?" exclaimed Miss P——. "Well, go away, if you do not wish to stay!" and she opened the door; but the cat, instead of going, recommenced running to and fro between the door and her friend, continuing to mew as she looked up into her face.

Miss P——'s attention was now attracted by a peculiar noise, as if proceeding from the outside of one of the windows on the ground-floor. A few moments more convinced her that some persons were attempting to force an entrance.

Instantly throwing a shawl around her, she hurried along the passage, the cat gliding by her side, purring now in evident contentment, to Lord ——'s bed-room door, where her knock was quickly answered, and an explanation given.

The household was soon aroused; bells were rung, lights flitted about, servants hurried here and there; and persons watching from the windows distinctly saw several men making off with all speed, and scrambling over an adjacent wall.

It was undoubtedly owing to the sagacity of the cat that the mansion was preserved from midnight robbery, and the inmates probably from some fearful outrage. She must have reasoned that the intruders had no business there; whilst her reason and affection combined induced her to warn her best friend of the threatened danger. She may have feared, also, that any one else in the house would have driven her heedlessly away.

My dear reader, may we not believe that this reasoning power was given to the dumb animal for the protection of the family against evil-doers? I might give you many instances of beneficent purposes being carried out by equally simple and apparently humble agencies.

Let us, then, learn always to treat dumb animals with kindness and consideration, since they are so often given to us as companions for our benefit. Like the cat, you may by vigilance be of essential service to others more powerful than yourself. For the same reason, never despise the good-will or warnings of even the most humble.

THE CAT WHICH RANG THE BELL.

I HAVE heard of another cat, who, had she lived in Lord ——'s house when attacked by robbers, might very speedily have aroused the family.

This cat, however, lived in a nunnery in France. She had observed that when a certain bell was rung, all the inmates assembled for their meals, when she also received her food.

One day she was shut up in a room by herself when she heard the bell ring. In vain she attempted to get out; she could not open the door, the window was too high to reach. At length, after some hours' imprisonment, the door was opened. Off she hurried to the place where she expected to find her dinner, but none was there. She was very hungry, and hunger is said to sharpen the wits. She knew where the rope hung which pulled the bell in the

THE CAT WHICH RANG THE BELL

belfry. " Now, when that bell rings I generally get my supper," she thought, as she ran towards the rope. It hung down temptingly within her reach—a good thick rope. She sprang upon it. It gave a pleasant tinkle. She jerked harder and harder, and the bell rang louder and louder. " Now I shall get my supper, though I have lost my dinner," she thought as she pulled away.

The nuns hearing the bell ring at so unusual an hour, came hurrying into the belfry, wondering what was the matter, when what was their surprise to see the cat turned bell-ringer ! They puzzled their heads for some time, till the lay sister who generally gave the cat her meals recollected that she had not been present at dinner-time ; and thus the mystery was solved, and Pussy rewarded for her exertions by having her supper brought to her without delay.

Instead of sitting down and crying when in a difficulty, think, like sensible Pussy, of the best way to get out of it. In lieu of *wringing* your hands, RING THE BELL.

THE AFFECTIONATE CAT THAT COULD MEASURE TIME.

THE last story reminds me of Mrs. F——'s account of the cat and the knocker. That same intelligent little cat was also one of the most affectionate of her race. Her young mistress used to go to school for a few hours daily in the neighbouring town. Pussy would every morning sally forth with her, and bound along beside her pony as far as the gate, then going quietly back to the house. Regularly, however, at the time the little girl was expected to return, the faithful pet might be seen watching about the door; and if Missy were delayed longer than usual, would extend her walk to the gate, there awaiting her approach, and evincing her delight by joyful gambols as soon as she descried her coming along the road. Pussy would then hurry back to the house-door, that she might give notice of her young mistress's return, and the moment she alighted would welcome her with happy purrings and caresses.

Endeavour to be as regular in all your ways as my friend's cat. Never keep your friends waiting for you, but rather wait for them. Show your affection and wish to please in this as in other ways. Thank Pussy for the excellent example she has set you.

THE CAT AND THE PRISONER.

WHILE speaking of the affection of cats, I must not forget to mention a notable example of it shown by the favourite cat of a young nobleman in the days of Queen Elizabeth.

For some political offence he had been shut up in prison, and had long pined in solitude, when he was startled by hearing a slight noise in the chimney. On looking up, great was his surprise and delight to see his favourite cat bound over the hearth towards him, purring joyfully at the meeting. She had probably been shut up for some time before she had made her escape, and then she must have sought her master, traversing miles of steep and slippery roofs, along dangerous parapets, and through forests of chimney-stacks, urged on by the strength of her attachment, and guided by a mysterious instinct, till she discovered the funnel which led into his prison chamber.

Certainly it was not by chance she made the discovery, nor was it exactly reason that conducted her to the spot. By whatever means she found it, we must regard the affectionate little creature as the very " Blondel of cats."

Never spare trouble or exertion to serve a friend, or to please those you are bound to please. Remember the prisoner's cat.

THE CAT AND THE HAWK.

Cats often show great courage, especially in defence of their young.

A cat had led her kittens out into the sunshine, and while they were frisking around her they were espied by a hawk soaring overhead. Down pounced the bird of prey and seized one in his talons. Encumbered by the weight of the fat little creature, he was unable to rise again before the mother cat had discovered what had occurred. With a bound she fiercely attacked the marauder, and compelled him to drop her kitten in order to defend himself. A regular combat now commenced, the hawk fighting with beak and talons, and rising occasionally on his wings. It seemed likely that he would thus gain the victory; still more when he struck his sharp beak into one of Pussy's eyes, while he tore her ears into shreds with his talons. At length, however, she managed what had been from the

THE CAT AND THE HAWK.

first her aim—to break one of her adversary's wings. She now sprang on him with renewed fury, and seizing him by the neck, quickly tore off his head. This done, regardless of her own sufferings, she began to lick the bleeding wounds of her kitten, and then, calling to its brothers and sisters, she carried it back to their secure home.

You will find many hawks with which you must do battle. The fiercest and most dangerous are those you must encounter every day. Huge dark-winged birds of prey— passionate temper, hatred, discontent, jealousy;—an ugly list, I will not go on with it. Fight against them as bravely as Pussy fought with the hawk which tried to carry off her kitten.

THE BENEVOLENT CAT.

THAT we must attribute to cats the estimable virtue of benevolence, Mrs. F—— gives me two anecdotes to prove.

A lady in the south of Ireland having lost a pet cat, and searched for it in vain, after four days was delighted to hear that it had returned. Hastening to welcome the truant with a wassail-bowl of warm milk in the kitchen, she observed another cat skulking with the timidity of an uninvited guest in an obscure corner. The pet cat received the caresses of its mistress with its usual pleasure, but, though it circled round the bowl of milk with grateful pur- rings, it declined to drink, going up to the stranger instead, whom, with varied mewings, "like man's own speech," it prevailed on to quit the shadowy background and approach the tempting food. At length both came up to the bowl, when the thirsty stranger feasted to its full satisfaction, while the cat of the house stood by in evident satisfaction watching its guest; and not until it would take no more could the host be persuaded to wet its whiskers in the tempting beverage.

Ever think of others before yourself. Attend first to their wants. Do not be outdone in true courtesy by a cat.

THE CAT AND HER MANY GUESTS.

MRS. F—— vouches for the following account, showing the hospitable disposition of cats. It was given to her by a clergyman, who had it direct from a friend.

A gentleman in Australia had a pet cat to which he daily gave a plate of viands with his own hands. The allowance was liberal, and there was always a remainder; but after some time the gentleman perceived that another cat came to share the repast. Finding that this occurred for several consecutive days, he increased the allowance. It was then found to be too much for two; there was again a residue for several days, when a third cat was brought in to share the feast. Amused at this proceeding, the gentleman now began to experiment, and again increased the daily dole of food. A fourth guest now appeared; and he continued adding gradually to the allowance of viands, and found that the number of feline guests also progressively increased, until about thirty were assembled; after which no further additions took place, so that he concluded that all those who lived within *visiting distance* were included:

indeed, the wonder was that so many could assemble, as the district he lived in was far from populous.

The stranger cats always decorously departed after dinner was over, leaving their hospitable entertainer, no doubt, with such grateful demonstrations as might be dictated by the feline code of etiquette.

Ask yourselves if you are always as anxious as was the Australian cat to invite your companions to enjoy with you the good things you have given you by kind friends. Ah! what an important lesson we may learn from this anecdote: always to think of others before ourselves. When young friends visit you, do you try your utmost to entertain them, thinking of their comfort before your own? Such is the lesson taught us by this cat, which gathered others of her kind to share the bounties provided by her kind master.

THE DISHONEST CAT.

I AM sorry to say that cats are not always so amiable as those I have described, but will occasionally play all sorts of tricks, like some dishonest boys and girls, to obtain what they want.

An Angora cat, which lived in a large establishment in France, had discovered that when a certain bell rang the cook always left the kitchen. Numerous niceties were scattered about, some on the tables and dressers, others before the fire. Pussy crept towards them, and tasted them; they exactly suited her palate. When she heard the cook's step returning, off she ran to a corner and pre-

THE DISHONEST CAT

tended to be sleeping soundly. How she longed that the bell would ring again!

At last, like another cat I have mentioned, she thought that she would try to ring it herself, and get cook out of the way; she could resist her longing for those sweet creams no longer. Off she crept, jumped up at the bell-rope, and succeeded in sounding the bell. Away hurried cook to answer it. The coast was now clear, and Pussy revelled in the delicacies left unguarded—being out of the kitchen, or apparently asleep in her corner, before cook returned.

This trick continued to answer Pussy's object for some time, the cook wondering what had become of her tarts and creams, till a watch was wisely set to discover the thief, when the dishonest though sagacious cat was seen to pull the bell, and then, when cook went out, to steal into the kitchen and feast at her leisure.

There is a proverb—which pray condemn as a bad one, because the motive offered is wrong—that "honesty is the best policy." Rather say, "Be honest because it is right." Pussy, with her manœuvres to steal the creams, thought herself very clever, but she was found out.

<hr />

PUSSY AND THE CREAM-JUG.

I MUST now tell you of another cat which was a sad thief, and showed a considerable amount of sagacity in obtaining what she wanted. One day she found a cream-jug on the

PUSSY AND THE CREAM-JUG.

breakfast-table, full of cream.   It was tall, and had a narrow mouth.   She longed for the nice rich contents, but could not reach the cream even with her tongue ; if she upset the jug, her theft would be discovered.   At last she thought to herself, " I may put in my paw, though I cannot get in my head, and some of that nice stuff will stick to it."

She made the experiment, and found it answer.   Licking her paw as often as she drew it out, she soon emptied the jug, so that when the family came down they had no cream for breakfast.   A few drops on the table-cloth, however, showed how it had been stolen—Pussy, like human beings who commit dishonest actions, not being quite so clever as she probably thought herself.

THE REVENGEFUL CAT.

CATS often show that they possess some of the vices as well as some of the virtues of human beings.   The tom-cat is frequently fierce, treacherous, and vindictive, and at no time can his humour be crossed with impunity.   Mrs. F—— mentions several instances of this.

A person she knew in the south of Ireland had severely chastised his cat for some misdemeanour, when the creature immediately ran off and could not be found.   Some days afterwards, as this person was going from home, what should he see in the centre of a narrow path between walls but his cat, with its back up, its eyeballs glaring, and a wicked expression in its countenance.   Expecting to frighten off the creature, he slashed at it with his handkerchief, when it sprang at him with a fierce hiss, and, seizing his hand in its mouth, held on so tightly that he was unable to beat it off. He hastened home, nearly fainting with the agony he endured, and not till the creature's body was cut from the head could the mangled hand be extricated.

An Irish gentleman had an only son, quite a little boy, who, being without playmates, was allowed to have a number of cats sleeping in his room. One day the boy beat the father of the family for some offence, and when he was asleep at night the revengeful beast seized him by the throat, and might have killed him had not instant help been at hand. The cat sprang from the window and was no more seen.

If you are always gentle and kind, you will never arouse anger or revenge. It may be aroused in the breast of the most harmless-looking creatures and the most contemptible. Your motive, however, for acting gently and lovingly should be, not fear of the consequences of a contrary behaviour, but that the former is right.

CHAPTER II.

Dogs.

WE now come to the noble Dog, indued by the Creator with qualities which especially fit him to be the companion of man. Such he is in all parts of the world; and although wild dogs exist, they appear, like savage human beings, to have retrograded from a state of civilization. The mongrels and curs, too, have evidently deteriorated, and lost the characteristic traits of their nobler ancestors.

What staunch fidelity, what affection, what courage, what devotion and generosity does the dog exhibit! Judged by the anecdotes I am about to narrate of him—a few only of the numberless instances recorded of his wonderful powers of mind—he must, I think, be considered the most sagacious of all animals, the mighty elephant not excepted.

THE DOG ROSSWELL.

I WILL begin with some anecdotes which I am myself able to authenticate.

Foremost must stand the noble Rosswell, who belonged to some connections of mine. He was of great size—a giant of the canine race—of a brown and white colour, one of his parents having seen the light in the frozen regions of Greenland, among the Esquimaux.

Rosswell, though a great favourite, being too large to be fed in the house, had his breakfast, consisting of porridge, in a large wooden bowl with a handle, sent out to him every morning, and placed close to a circular shrubbery before the house. Directly it arrived, he would cautiously put his nose to the bowl, and if, as was generally the case, the contents were too hot for his taste, he would take it up by the handle and walk with it round the shrubbery at a dignified pace, putting it down again at the same spot. He would then try the porridge once more, and if it were still too hot he would again take up the bowl and walk round and round as before, till he was satisfied that the super-abundant caloric had been dissipated, when, putting it down, he would leisurely partake of his meal.

Everything he did was in the same methodical, civilized fashion. One of the ladies of the family had dropped a valuable bracelet during a walk. In the evening Rosswell entered the house and proceeded straight up to her with his mouth firmly closed. "What have you got there?" she asked, when he at once opened his huge mouth and revealed the missing bracelet.

The same lady was fond of birds, and had several young ones brought to her from time to time to tame. Rosswell must have observed this. One day he appeared again with his mouth closed, and came up to her. On opening his jaws, which he allowed her to do, what was her surprise to see within them a little bird, perfectly unhurt! After this he very frequently brought her birds in his mouth, which he had caught without in any way injuring them.

He had another strange fancy. It was to catch hedge-hogs; but, instead of killing them, he invariably brought them into the house and placed them before the kitchen fire—supposing, apparently, that they enjoyed its warmth.

With two of the ladies of the family he was a great favourite, and used to romp with them to his heart's content. The youngest, however, being of a timid disposition, could never get over a certain amount of terror with which his first appearance had inspired her.

At length Rosswell disappeared. Although inquiries were everywhere made for him he could not be found. It was suspected that he had been stolen, with the connivance of one of the domestics, who owed him a grudge. Weeks passed away, and all hope of recovering Rosswell had been abandoned, when one day he rushed into the house, looking lean and gaunt, with a broken piece of rope hanging to his neck, showing that he had been kept "in durance vile," and had only just broken his bonds. The two elder sisters he greeted with the most exuberant marks of affection, leaping up and trying to lick their faces; but directly the youngest appeared he slowly crept forward, lay down at her feet, wagging his tail, and glancing up at her countenance with an unmistakably gentle look.

Rosswell, not without provocation, had taken a dislike to a little dog belonging to Captain ——; and at last, having been annoyed beyond endurance, he gave the small cur a bite which sent it yelping away. Captain —— was passing at the time, and, angry at the treatment his dog had received, declared that he would shoot Rosswell if it ever happened again. Knowing that Captain —— would certainly fulfil his threat, the elder lady, who was of determined character, and instigated by regard for Rosswell, called the dog to her, and began belabouring him with a stout stick, pronouncing the name of the little dog all the time. Rosswell received the castigation with the utmost humility ; and from that day forward avoided the little dog, never retaliating when annoyed, and hanging down his head when its name was mentioned.

Rosswell had a remarkable liking for sugar-plums, and would at all times prefer a handful to a piece of meat. If, however, a pile of them were placed between his paws, and he was told that they were for baby, he would not touch them, but watch with wagging tail while the little fellow picked them up. He might probably have objected had any one else attempted to take them away.

Gallant Rosswell!—he fell a victim at length to the wicked hatred of his old enemy the cook, who mixed poison with his food, which destroyed his life.

Rosswell's mistresses mourned for him, as I daresay you will ; but they did not seek to punish the wicked woman as she deserved.

What a noble fellow he was, how submissive under castigation, how gentle when he saw that his boisterous behaviour frightened his youngest mistress, how obedient to command, how strict in the performance of his duty ! And what self-restraint did he exercise ! Think of him with baby's sugar-plums between his paws—not one would he touch.

My reader, let me ask you one question : Are you as firm in resisting temptation as was gallant Rosswell ? He acted rightly through instinct ; but you have the power to discern between good and evil, aided by the counsels of your kind friends.   Do not shame the teaching of your parents by acting in any manner unworthy of yourself.

TYROL, THE DOG WHICH RANG THE BELL.

I HAVE told you of several cats which rang bells.   Another connection of mine, living in the Highlands, had a dog called Tyrol.   He had been taught to do all sorts of things. Among others, to fetch his master's slippers at bed-time ; and when told that fresh peat was required for the fire, away he would go to the peat-basket and bring piece after piece, till a sufficient quantity had been piled up.

He had also learned to pull the bell-rope to summon the servant.   This he could easily accomplish at his own home, where the rope was sufficiently long for him to reach ; but on one occasion he accompanied his master on a visit to a friend's house, where he was desired to exhibit his various accomplishments.   When told to ring the bell, he made several attempts in vain.   The end of the rope was too high up for him to reach.   At length, what was the surprise of all present to see him seize a chair by the leg, and pull it up to the wall, when, jumping up, he gave the rope a hearty tug, evidently very much to his own satisfaction.

You will generally find that, difficult as a task may seem, if you seek for the right means you may accomplish it. Drag the chair up to the bell-rope which you cannot otherwise reach.

THE SHEPHERD'S DOG AND THE LOST CHILD.

I AM sorry that I do not know the name of a certain shepherd's dog, but which deserves to be recorded in letters of gold.

His master, who had charge of a flock which fed among the Grampian Hills, set out from home one day accompanied by his little boy, scarcely more than four years old. The children of Scottish shepherds begin learning their future duties at an early age. The day, bright at first, passed on, when a thick mist began to rise, shrouding the surrounding country. The shepherd, seeing this, hurried onward to collect his scattered flock, calling his dog to his assistance, and leaving his little boy at a spot where he believed that he should easily find him again. The fog grew thicker and thicker; and so far had the flock rambled, that some time passed before they could be collected together.

On his return to look for his child, the darkness had increased so much that he could not discover him. The anxious father wandered on, calling on his child—but no answer came; his dog, too, had disappeared. He had himself lost his way. At length the moon rose, when he discovered that he was not far from his own cottage. He hastened towards it, hoping that the child had reached it before him; but the little boy had not appeared, nor had the dog been seen.   The agony of the parents can be better imagined than described.   No torches were to be procured, and the shepherd had to wait till daylight ere he could set out with a companion or two to assist him in his search.   All day he searched in vain.   On his return, sick at heart, at nightfall, he heard that his dog had appeared during the day, received his accustomed meal of a bannock, and then scampered off at full speed across the moor, being out of sight before any one could follow him.

All night long the father waited, expecting the dog to return ; but the animal not appearing, he again, as soon as it was daylight, set off on his search.   During his absence, the dog hurried up to the cottage, as on the previous day, and went off again immediately he had received his bannock.

At last, after this had occurred on two more successive days, the shepherd resolved to remain at home till his dog should appear, and then to follow him.

The sagacious animal appearing as before, at once understood his master's purpose, and instead of scampering off at full speed, kept in sight as he led the way across the moor.   It was then seen that he held in his mouth the larger portion of the cake which had been given him.   The dog conducted the shepherd to a cataract which fell roaring and foaming amid rocks into a ravine far down below.   Descending an almost perpendicular cliff, the dog entered a cavern, close in front of which the seething torrent passed. The shepherd with great difficulty made his way to it, when, as he reached the entrance, he saw his child, unhurt,

THE SHEPHERD'S DOG AND THE LOST CHILD.

seated on the ground eating the cake brought by the dog, who stood watching his young charge thus occupied, with a proud consciousness of the important duty he had undertaken.

The father, embracing his child, carried him up the steep ascent, down which it appeared he had scrambled in the dark, happily reaching the cave. This he had been afraid to quit on account of the torrent; and here the dog by his scent had traced him, remaining with him night and day, till, conscious that food was as necessary for the child as for himself, he had gone home to procure him some of his own allowance.

Thus the faithful animal had, by a wonderful exercise of his reasoning power, preserved the child's life.

MY DOG ALP.

A DEAR friend gave me, many years ago, a rough, white terrier puppy, which I called Alp. I fed him with my own hand from the first, and he consequently evinced the warmest attachment to me. No animal could be more obedient; and he seemed to watch my every look to ascertain what I wished him to do.

The expression of his countenance showed his intelligence; and whenever I talked to him he seemed to be making the most strenuous efforts to reply, twisting about his lips in a fashion which often made me burst into a fit of laughter, when he would give a curious bark of delight, as much as to say,—"Ay, I can utter as meaning a sound as that."

I felt very sure that no burglar would venture into the house while he was on the watch.

I never beat him in his life; but once I pretended to do so, with a hollow reed which happened to be in the room, on his persisting, contrary to my orders, in lying down on the rug before the fire whenever my back was turned. As I was about to leave the room, I placed the reed on the rug, and admonished him to be careful. On my return, some time afterwards, I found the reed torn up into the most minute shreds. On looking round, I saw Alp in the furthest corner of the room, twisting his mouth, wriggling about, and wagging his tail, while every now and then he turned furtive glances towards the rug, telling me as plainly as if he could speak,—" I could not resist the temptation—I did it, I own—but don't be angry with me. You see I have now got as far away from the rug as I could be." Alp, seeing me laugh, rushed from his corner to lick my hand. He ever afterwards, however, avoided the rug.

For his size, he was the best swimmer and diver among dogs I ever saw. He would, without hesitation, plunge into water six or eight feet deep, and bring up a stone from the bottom almost as big as his head, or dash forth from the sea-beach and boldly breast the foaming billows of the Atlantic.

After seeing what Alp did do, and feeling sure of what he could have done had circumstances called forth his powers, I am ready to believe the accounts I have heard of the wonderful performances of others of his race.

A young Newfoundland dog, living in Glasgow a few

years ago, acted, under similar circumstances, very much as Alp did. As he sometimes misbehaved himself, a whip was kept near him, which was occasionally applied to his back. He naturally took a dislike to this article, and more than once was found with it in his mouth, moving slyly towards the door.

Being shut up at night in the house to watch it, he in his rounds discovered the detested instrument of punishment. To get rid of it, he attempted to thrust it under the door. It stuck fast, however, by the thick end. A few nights afterwards he again got hold of the whip, and persevered till he shoved through the thick end, when some one passing by carried it off. On being questioned as to what had become of the whip, he betrayed his guilt by his looks, and slunk away with his tail between his legs.

THE DOG AND THE THIEF.

A GENTLEMAN who lived near Stirling, possessed a powerful mastiff. One evening, as he was going his rounds through the grounds, he observed a man with a sack on his back suspiciously proceeding towards the orchard. The dog followed, crouching down while the man filled his sack with apples. The dog waited till the thief had thrown the heavy sack over his shoulders, holding on to the mouth with both hands. When the man was thus unable to defend himself, the dog rushed forward and stood in front of him, barking loudly for assistance, and leaving him the option of dropping his plunder and fighting for life and liberty, or of being captured.   Paralyzed with fear, he stood still, till the servants coming from the house made him prisoner.

Be calm and cool in the face of a foe—remonstrate with a wrong-doer—fly from tempters ; but you cannot be too eager and violent in attacking temptation immediately it presents itself.

THE CLEANLY DOG.

A FRIEND told me of another dog, which had been taught habits of cleanliness that some young gentlemen, accustomed to enter the drawing-room with dirty shoes, might advantageously imitate.   A shallow tub of water was placed in the hall, near the front door.   Whenever this well-behaved dog came into the house, if the roads were muddy from rain, or dusty from dry weather, he used to run to the tub and wash his feet—drying them, it is to be presumed, on the door-mat—before venturing into any of the sitting-rooms to which he had admission.

MASTER ROUGH.

HAVING mentioned this cleanly dog, I must next introduce to you a canine friend, called Master Rough, belonging to my kind next-door neighbours ; and I think you will acknowledge that he surpasses the other in the propriety of his behaviour.

Master Rough is very small, and his name describes his

appearance. As I hear his voice, I might suppose him to be somewhat ill-natured, did I not know that his bark is worse than his bite. He is only indignant at being told by his mistress to do something he dislikes; but he does it notwithstanding, though he has, it must be confessed, a will of his own, like some young folks. He does not often soil his dainty feet by going out into the muddy road; but when he does, on his return he carefully wipes them on the door-mat.

At meal-times he goes to a cupboard, in which is kept a bowl and napkin for his especial use. The napkin he first spreads on the carpet, and then placing the bowl in the centre, barks to give notice that his table is ready. After this, he sits down and waits patiently till his dinner is put into the bowl, on which he falls to and gobbles it up,—the table-cloth preventing any of the bits which tumble over from soiling the carpet. It has been asserted that he wipes his mouth afterwards in the napkin; but I suspect that he is merely picking up the bits outside. I am sorry to say that he forgets to fold up his table-cloth neatly and to put it away, which he certainly should do; nor can he be persuaded to wash out his bowl, though he does not object to lick it clean. People and dogs, however, have different ways of doing things, and Master Rough chooses to follow his way, and is perfectly satisfied with himself—like some young folks, who may not, however, be right for all that.

His principal other accomplishment is to carry up the newspaper, after it has been read by the gentleman downstairs, to his mistress in the drawing-room, when he receives a cake as his reward. He also may be seen carrying a basket after his mistress, with a biscuit in it, which he knows will be his in due time ; but that if be misbehaves himself by gobbling it greedily up—as he has sometimes done, I hear—he will have to carry the basket without the biscuit ; so having learned wisdom from experience, he now patiently waits till it is given to him.

If Master Rough is not so clever as some dogs I have to tell you about, he does his best in most respects ; and I am very sure that no thief would venture to break into the house in which he keeps watch : so that he makes himself —what all boys and girls should strive to be—very useful.

BYRON, THE NEWFOUNDLAND DOG.

NEXT on my list of canine favourites stands a noble New-foundland dog named Byron, which belonged to the father of my friend, Mrs. F——. On one occasion he accompanied the family to Dawlish, on the coast of Devonshire. His kennel was at the back of the house. Whenever his master was going out, the servant loosened Byron, who immediately ran round, never entering the house, and joined him, accompanying him in his walk.

One day, after getting some way from home, his master found that he had forgotten his walking-stick. He showed the dog his empty hands, and pointed towards the house. Byron, instantly comprehending what was wanted, set off, and made his way into the house by the front door, through which he had never before passed. In the hall was a hat-stand with several walking-sticks in it. Byron, in his eagerness, seized the first he could reach, and carried it joyfully to his master. It was not the right one, however. Mr. —— on this patted him on the head, gave him back the stick, and again pointed towards the house. The dog, apparently considering for a few moments what mistake he could have made, ran home again, and exchanged the stick for the one his master usually carried. After this, he had the walking-stick given him to carry, an office of which he seemed very proud.

One day while thus employed, following his master with stately gravity, he was annoyed during the whole time by a little yelping cur jumping up at his ears. Byron shook his head, and growled a little from time to time, but took no further notice, and never offered to lay down the stick to punish the offender.

On reaching the beach, Mr. —— threw the stick into the waves for the dog to bring it out. Then, to the amusement of a crowd of bystanders, Byron, seizing his troublesome and pertinacious tormentor by the back of the neck, plunged with him into the foaming water, where he ducked him well several times, and then allowed him to find his way out as best he could ; while he himself, mindful of his duty, swam onward in search of the now somewhat distant walking-stick, which he brought to his master's feet with his usual calm demeanour. The little cur never again troubled him.

Be not less magnanimous than Byron, when troublesome boys try to annoy you whilst you are performing your duties ; but employ gentle words instead of duckings to silence them. Drown the yelping curs—bad thoughts, unamiable tempers, temptations, and such like—which assault you from within.

THE NEWFOUNDLAND DOG AND THE MARKED SHILLING.

I MUST now tell you a story which many believe, but which others consider "too good to be true."

A gentleman who owned a fine Newfoundland dog, of which he was very proud, was one warm summer's evening riding out with a friend, when he asserted that his dog would find and bring to him any article he might leave behind him. Accordingly it was agreed that a shilling should be marked and placed under a stone, and that after they had proceeded three or four miles on their road, the dog should be sent back for it. This was done—the dog, which was with them, observing them place the coin under the stone, a somewhat heavy one. They then rode forward the distance proposed, when the dog was despatched by his master for the shilling. He seemed fully to understand what was required of him; and the two gentlemen reached home, expecting the dog to follow immediately. They waited, however, in vain. The dog did not make his appearance, and they began to fear that some accident had happened to the animal.

The faithful dog was, however, obedient to his master's orders. On reaching the stone he found it too heavy to lift, and while scraping and working away, barking every now and then in his eagerness, two horsemen came by. Observing the dog thus employed, one of them dismounted and turned over the stone, fancying that some creature had taken refuge beneath it. As he did so, his eye fell on the coin, which—not suspecting that it was the object sought for —he put into his breeches pocket before the animal could get hold of it. Still wondering what the dog wanted, he remounted his steed, and with his companion rode rapidly on to an inn nearly twenty miles off, where they purposed passing the night.

The dog, which had caught sight of the shilling as it was transferred to the stranger's pocket, followed them closely, and watched the sleeping-room into which they were shown. He must have observed them take off their clothes, and seen the man who had taken possession of the shilling hang his breeches over the back of a chair. Waiting till the travellers were wrapped in slumber, he seized the garment in his mouth —being unable to abstract the shilling—and bounded out of the window, nor stopped till he reached his home. His master was awakened early in the morning by hearing the dog barking and scratching at his door. He was greatly surprised to find what he had brought, and more so to discover not only the marked shilling, but a watch and purse besides. As he had no wish that his dog should act the thief, or that he himself should become the receiver of stolen goods, he advertised the articles which had been carried off; and after some time the owner appeared, when all that had occurred was explained.

The only way to account for the dog not at first seizing the shilling is, that grateful for the assistance afforded him in removing the stone, he supposed that the stranger was about to give him the coin, and that he only discovered his

THE NEWFOUNDLAND DOG AND THE MARKED SHILLING

mistake when it was too late. His natural gentleness and
generosity may have prevented him from attacking the
man and trying to obtain it by force.

Patiently and perseveringly follow up the line of duty
which has been set you. When I see a boy studying hard
at his lessons, or doing his duty in any other way, I can
say, "Ah, he is searching for the marked shilling; and I
am sure he will find it."

THE LOST KEYS.

MANY species of dogs appear, like the last mentioned, to be
especially indued with the faculty of distinguishing their
master's property, and to possess the desire of restoring it
to them when lost.

Mrs. F—— told me of an instance of this with which
she was acquainted. A gentleman residing in the county
of Cork, finding his out-houses infested by rats, sent for
four small terriers to extirpate them. He amused himself
with teaching the dogs a variety of canine accomplishments,—among others, to fetch and carry whatever he
sent them for.

Returning one day from his daily walk, he discovered
that a bunch of keys which he supposed was in his pocket
was not there. Hoping that he might have left them at
home, he made diligent search everywhere, but in vain.
One of the little terriers had observed his master thus
searching about, and there can be no doubt that, after
pondering the matter in his mind, he came to the con-

clusion that something was lost. Be that as it may, off
he set by himself from the house, and after the lapse of
some hours up he came running with eager delight, the
lost keys dangling from his mouth, and jingling loudly as
he gambolled about in his happiness. He then dropped
them at his master's feet.

We may be sure that the dog was well caressed, and became from thenceforward the prime favourite.

That terrier was a little dog, but still he was of much
use, not only by killing rats, which was his regular duty,
but by trying to find out what his master wanted to have
done, and doing it.

Little boys and girls may be of still greater use, if they
will both perform *their* regular duties, and try to find out
what there is to be done, and then, like the terrier, do it.

THE DOG WHICH ACTED AS CONSTABLE.

MRS. F—— told me another anecdote, which illustrates the
fidelity and reasoning power so frequently exhibited by the
shepherd's dog.

About the year 1827, her father sold some lambs to a
butcher in Melrose, who took them away in his cart. Their
shepherd had a young dog in training at the time. Shortly
after the sale of the lambs he missed this dog, and hastened
in search of him.

On reaching the chain bridge which is thrown over the
river for the use of foot-passengers, he was told that the
dog had been seen standing on it watching the butcher's

cart containing the lambs, which was crossing the ford beneath. As soon as it had gained the other bank the dog followed it to Melrose. The shepherd pursued the supposed truant till he reached the town, where in front of the butcher's shop stood the cart with the lambs still in it, and the dog standing like a constable by it, threatening every one who approached to unload it.

He had evidently considered that the animals were stolen, and that it was his duty to keep watch over them. When, however, his master appeared, and called him away, he seemed at once to understand that all was right, and followed him willingly.

Be watchful over whatever is committed to your charge, and be equally watchful over yourself.

THE LOST CHILD RECOVERED.

In the backwoods of North America lived a settler and his family, far away from towns and villages. The children of such families at an early age learn to take care of themselves, and fearlessly wander to a distance from home to gather wild fruits, to fish in the streams, or to search for maple-trees from which to extract sugar in the autumn.

One evening the rest of the boys and girls had come in from their various occupations, except the youngest, a little fellow of four or five years old. One of his brothers thought he had gone with Silas, and Silas fancied that he was with James and Mary, but neither of them till then

THE LOST CHILD RECOVERED.

had missed him. The whole family, thrown into a state of consternation, hurried out with torches, for it was now getting dark, and shouted for him, and searched round and round the clearing far and wide, but he was nowhere to be found. I need not describe their feelings. The next morning they set forth again, searching still further. All day they were so employed, but in vain. They began to fear that poor little Marcus had been killed by a rattlesnake, or that a bear had come and carried him off.

The next night was a sorrowful one for all the family. Once more they were preparing to set out, when a tall, copper-coloured Indian, habited in a dress of skins, was seen coming through the forest, followed by a magnificent blood-hound. He approached the settlers and inquired what was the matter. They told him, when he desired to see the socks and shoes last worn by the child. They were eagerly produced by the mother. The Indian showed them to his dog, at the same time patting him on the head. The animal evidently comprehended what his master required, and scenting about for a short time, began to bay loudly, then set off, without turning to the right or to the left, through the forest, followed by the Indian and the child's father and elder brothers. He was soon out of sight, but the Indian knew by the marks on the ground the way he had taken.

A long, long chase the hound led them, till he was seen bounding back with animation in his eye and a look which told that he had been successful in his search. The father and his sons hurried after the Indian, who closely followed his dog, and to their joy discovered little Marcus, pale and exhausted, but unhurt, with the dog standing over him.

He soon recovered, and told them how he had lost his way, and lived upon berries and other wild fruits till he had sunk down unable to go further. His life had undoubtedly been preserved by means of the sagacious blood-hound.

DOG WAKING UP SERVANTS.

I HAVE told you of Tyrol, who used to ring the bell; I will now describe another dog named Dash, who was still more clever. When any of the servants of the family had to sit up for their master or mistress, and fell asleep in their chair, scarcely would they have settled themselves when the parlour bell would be heard to ring. They were greatly puzzled to account for this, and in vain attempted to solve the mystery.

Dash was a black and white spaniel, who was generally considered a fairly clever dog, but not suspected of possessing any unusual amount of knowingness. He never failed, when his master told him to get anything, to find it and lay it at his feet. If one glove was missing, and the other shown to him, he was sure to hunt about till he discovered it.

One morning a person arrived with a letter before breakfast, to be delivered into the hands of Dash's master. The man was shown into the parlour, where he was about to sit down, when his ears were saluted by a growl, and there was Dash, seated in a chair near the fireplace. The dog

was within reach of the ring of the bell-pull, and whenever
the man attempted to sit down, Dash put up his paw on the
ring and growled again.   At length the stranger, curious to
see what the dog would do if he persevered, sat down in a
chair.   Dash, on this, instead of flying at the man, as some
stupid dogs would have done, pulled the bell-rope, and a
servant coming in on the summons, was greatly astonished
when the man told him that the dog had rung the bell.

Thus the mystery which had long puzzled him and his
fellow-servants was explained.   On comparing notes, they
recollected that whenever the bell sounded, Dash was not
to be seen ; and there could now be no doubt that immediately he observed them closing their eyes, he had hastened
off to the parlour, the bell-rope of which he could easily
reach, in order to rouse them to watchfulness.

In corroboration of this account, my friend Mrs. F——
mentioned the case of a Newfoundland dog, which was one
day accidentally shut up in the dining-room, when the
family were out.   He scratched at the door and whined
loudly for a length of time ; but though the servants heard
him, they paid no attention.   At length, as if the thought
had suddenly occurred to him that whenever the bell was
rung the door was opened, he actually rang the bell right
heartily.   A servant instantly obeyed the summons, when
out sprang the dog, wagging his tail with delight at the
result of his sagacious experiment, and leaving the man in
amazement at finding no person in the room.

THE SHEEP-DOG AND HIS MISTRESS'S CLOAK.

THERE are many instances of dogs showing attention to their owner's interests. Mr. Jesse mentions one which exhibits a wonderful power of reasoning in a dog.

The sheep-dog used to accompany the farm-servants about the farm, but ran home to be fed at the dinner-hour of his mistress, returning afterwards to his duty in the fields. One day, as he was approaching the house, he met a young woman, whom he had never before seen, leaving it wearing his mistress's cloak, which had in reality been lent her. Hungry as he was, he nevertheless turned about and followed closely at her heels, greatly to her alarm. Hurrying on, the dog still accompanied her, till she reached the house in which the brother of the dog's mistress resided, with whom he was well acquainted. On seeing the young woman enter it, the faithful animal turned about, and went quietly back to the farm. It was thus evident that, from seeing her go into a house which he knew, he was satisfied that she was a friend of the family. Had she gone to a strange place, he would probably have tried to take the cloak from her.

Follow what you believe to be the right course, like the faithful sheep-dog; and though the result may not answer your expectations, do not be disheartened. Persevere in acting rightly : the reward *will* come.

THE DOG AND THE MARE.

Dogs and horses frequently form friendships. A Newfoundland dog had attached himself to a mare belonging to his master, and seemed to consider himself especially the guardian of his less sagacious companion. Whenever the groom began to saddle the mare, the dog used to lie down with his nose between his paws, watching the proceeding. The moment the operation was finished, up jumped the dog, seized the reins in his mouth, and led the mare to her master, following him in his ride.

On returning home, the reins being again given to him, he would lead his friend back to the stable. If, on his arrival, the groom happened to be out of the way, he would bark vehemently till he made his appearance, and then hand over his charge to him.

You may be young and little, but if you exercise discretion and judgment, you may assist those much bigger and older than yourself. Learn from the dog, however, not to give yourself airs in consequence; you will have simply performed your duty in making yourself useful.

THE TWO DOGS AND THEIR CHARGE.

I must give you another anecdote somewhat similar to the last.

A little terrier, and another dog, equally faithful and sagacious, had attached themselves to their master's horse,

THE DOG AND THE MARE.

which they always accompanied when it went out.   If the master rode out on it to dinner, the two dogs used to remain contentedly in the stable with their friend, till it was required to carry its master home.

One night the gentleman had ordered his horse to be brought, but waited in vain for its appearance.   At length the groom was summoned, when he declared that he dared not take the horse out of the stable, as one of the dogs was on its back, and the other by its side, threatening to attack every person who came up to the animal.   The owner, observing that the groom was a stranger, suspected at once that the dogs would not trust him, and had himself to go round to the stable, when the faithful animals at once delivered their charge up to him.

CRIB THE BULL-TERRIER SAVING THE LIFE OF BOB THE SETTER.

Two dogs belonged to the family of Mrs. F——.   One, Bob, a black setter, who was, like most of his species, an excellent swimmer ; the other, Crib, a bull-terrier, who had no love for the water, and thought himself ill-used whenever he was compelled to take a bath.

Several of the family were walking along the bank of the Tweed, accompanied by the two dogs, when Bob, as usual, plunged into the water, but Crib kept close to their heels. The ladies happened to be in earnest conversation, and were taking no notice of the dogs, when their attention was attracted by a second plunge, and Bob was seen, apparently seized with cramp, floundering in the middle of the river, Crib swimming eagerly towards him. Bob sank just as his friend reached him, but Crib seized him by the nape of the neck in his powerful jaws, and thus swam with him to shore.

There existed no particular friendship between the dogs; and when Crib's natural aversion to the water is considered, it must be acknowledged that he well deserved the Humane Society's Medal for his gallantry.

It is truly a noble deed to save the life of a fellow-creature, though it but rarely falls to the lot of any one. But, though you may never have an opportunity of doing that, you may always find numerous ways of rendering assistance to those who may, in one form or other, be in want of it.

THE NEWFOUNDLAND DOG AND THE THIEVISH PORTER.

A GROCER owned a Newfoundland dog, which used frequently to take charge of the shop. While thus lying down with his nose between his paws, he observed one of the porters frequently visiting the till. He suspected that the man had no business to go there. He therefore watched him, and, following him, observed him hide the money he had taken in the stable. The dog, on this, attempted to lead several persons in whom he had confidence towards the place, by pulling in a peculiar manner at their clothes. They took no heed of him, till at length one of the apprentices going to the stable, the dog followed him and began scratching at a heap of rubbish in a corner.

The young man's attention being aroused, he watched the animal, which soon scratched up several pieces of money. The apprentice, collecting them, evidently to the dog's satisfaction, took them to his master, who marked them, and restored them to the place where they were discovered.

The porter, who for some other cause was suspected, was at length arrested, when some of the marked coin was found on him. On being taken before a magistrate, he confessed his guilt, and was convicted of the theft.

THE TERRIER AND THE DUCKLINGS.

A TERRIER, which lived at Dunrobin Castle many years ago, had a family of puppies, which were taken from her and drowned. How she mourned for her offspring, and wondered why her owner had been so cruel as to allow them to be carried away! Her maternal feelings were as strong as those of other creatures, and she felt a longing to exercise them. At length she caught sight of a brood of young ducklings. They were young, and required care just like her own dear little whelps; so, seizing them, she carried them off one by one to her kennel, and would allow no one to take them away. They seemed to understand that they had obtained a very good nurse, and she watched them with the most affectionate care. When, however, they made their way to the water and plunged in, she exhibited the greatest alarm, believing that they would be drowned, as her own puppies had been. No sooner had she reached the shore than she picked them up in her mouth, and carried

THE TERRIER AND THE DUCKLINGS.

them off to her kennel, resolving, probably, never to allow them to run into the same danger again.

After the ducklings grew up, and were no longer willing to submit to her canine style of nursing, she again became the mother of another litter.   On this also being destroyed, she seized two cock chickens, which she reared with the same care that she had done the ducklings.   When, however, the young cocks began to try their voices, their foster-mother was as much annoyed as she had been by the ducks going into the water, and invariably did her best to stop their crowing.

You will never want objects on which to exercise your kind feelings.   "The poor you have always with you."   You must not be disheartened or dissatisfied if they persist in following a different course from that which you think they ought to do.   How often, when a baby, have you cried lustily when your mother or nurse heartily wished you to be silent; and as you grew older, perversely ran away into danger when they called after you!   Through life remember that little terrier, and like her persevere in befriending those in need.

THE NEWFOUNDLAND DOG SAVING THE MASTIFF.

I MUST tell you one more anecdote of two dogs of a similar character to one I gave you a few pages back, but in this instance they were professed enemies.   It happened at Donaghadee, where a pier was in course of building.

Two dogs—one a Newfoundland, and the other a mastiff —were seen by several people engaged in a fierce and prolonged battle on the pier. They were both powerful dogs, and though good-natured when alone, were much in the habit of thus fighting whenever they met. At length they both fell into the sea, and as the pier was long and steep, they had no means of escape but by swimming a considerable distance. The cold bath brought the combat to an end, and each began to make for the land as best he could.

The Newfoundland dog speedily gained the shore, on which he stood shaking himself, at the same time watching the motions of his late antagonist, who, being no swimmer, began to struggle, and was just about to sink. On seeing this, in he dashed, took the other gently by the collar, kept his head above water, and brought him safely to land.

After this they became inseparable friends, and never fought again; and when the Newfoundland dog met his death by a stone waggon running over him, the mastiff languished, and evidently mourned for him for a long time.

Let this incident afford us great encouragement to love our enemies, and to return good for evil, since we find the feeling implanted in the breast of a dog to save the life of his antagonist, and to cherish him afterwards as a friend.

We may never be called on to save the life of a foe; but that would not be more difficult to our natural disposition than acting kindly and forgivingly towards those who daily annoy us—who injure us or offer us petty insults.

THE NEWFOUNDLAND PUNISHING THE LITTLE DOG.

You remember the way Byron punished his troublesome little assailant. Another Newfoundland dog, of a noble and generous disposition, was often assailed in the same way by noisy curs in the streets. He generally passed them with apparent unconcern, till one little brute ventured to bite him in the back of the leg. This was a degree of wanton insult which could not be patiently endured; so turning round, he ran after the offender, and seized him by the poll. In this manner he carried him to the quay, and holding him for some time over the water, at length dropped him into it. He did not, however, intend that the culprit should be drowned. Waiting till he was not only well ducked, but nearly sinking, he plunged in and brought him safely to land.

Could you venture to look a Newfoundland dog in the face, and call him a brute beast, if you feel that you have acted with less generosity than he exhibited!

THE TERRIER AND THE BANTAM.

Among the strange friendships existing between animals of different natures, I must mention one formed between a terrier and a bantam.

The little dog was suffering so severely from the distemper, that it was necessary to confine her to her kennel, which had open bars in front of it. A bantam cock which

THE TERRIER AND THE BANTAM.

lived in the yard, walking up and down, observed the poor little animal, and gazed at her with looks of deep compassion. At last he managed to squeeze himself through the bars. The terrier evidently understood his feelings, and from that day forward the bantam took up his abode in the dog's prison—like a brave physician, fearless of catching the complaint of his patient—and seldom left it, except to pick up his daily food. When he did so, the dog became uneasy, whining till her friend returned.

The terrier became worse, and the bantam redoubled his attentions, and, for the purpose of warming the dog, took his place between her fore-legs; and then the poor little invalid settled down on the bird, apparently to enjoy the warmth afforded by his feathers. Thus, day after day was passed in the closest bonds of affection, till the terrier died of the disease from which she had been suffering. The bantam appeared inconsolable at the loss of his friend, and it was some time before he recovered his usual spirits.

Imitate that little bantam. You will find very many human beings, in lieu of sick terriers, to nurse. As willingly as the bird gave up pleasant amusements, so rouse yourself from sloth for their sakes.

THE COMPASSIONATE DOG WHICH SAVED PUSSY'S LIFE.

I MUST give you another instance, still more curious than the former, of friendship between two animals.

A number of rough boys in Liverpool had stoned a cat,

and dragged it through a pool of water, no one of the many passers-by attempting to stop them ; when a dog coming up was moved with pity and indignation at the brutal proceedings, which ought to have induced the human beings who witnessed it to interfere. Barking furiously, he rushed in among the boys, and then carried off the ill-used cat in his mouth, bleeding, and almost senseless, to his kennel at the Talbot Inn, to which he belonged. He there laid it on the straw, licked it till it was clean, and then stretched himself on it, as if to impart to it some of his own warmth. On its beginning to revive, he set out to obtain food for it, when the people of the inn, noticing his behaviour, gave his patient some warm milk.

Some days passed before the cat recovered, and during the whole time the dog never remitted in his attentions to it. The cat, in return, exhibited the warmest gratitude to the dog, and for many years afterwards they were seen going about the streets of Liverpool together.

Do you not blush for human nature when you hear of boys exhibiting less compassion than a dog? Be watchful that you never have cause to blush for yourself.

FOP PLAYING AT HIDE-AND-SEEK.

NOT only can dogs be taught all sorts of amusing tricks, but they can play intelligently at games themselves. Mrs. Lee tells us of a fox-terrier named Fop, who used to hide his eyes, and suffer those playing with him to conceal themselves before he looked up. I should have liked to see jolly Fop at his sports.   If his playfellow hid himself behind a curtain, Fop would go carefully past that particular curtain, looking behind the others and the rest of the furniture, and when he thought he had looked long enough, seize the concealing curtain, and drag it aside in triumph.

The drollest thing, however, was to see him take his turn at hiding.   He would get under a chair, and fancy he could not be seen.   Of course, those at play with him pretended not to know where he was hiding, and it was most amusing to witness his agitation as they passed.

Once Fop was ill, and had taken some homœopathic globules, which were supposed to have cured him.   Afterwards, when anything was the matter with him, he would stand near the medicine-box, and hold his mouth open to receive a pill.   He possibly might have had a taste for sugar-plums.

Professor Owen tells us of another dog which was taught by his master to play at hide-and-seek.   When he heard the words, " Let us have a game," he immediately hid his eyes between his paws in the most honourable manner; and when his owner had placed a sixpence or a piece of cake in the most improbable place, he started up, and invariably found it.

Young dogs, it may thus be seen, enjoy games of play as much as boys and girls do, and romping still more so.

THE SPANIEL AND HIS FRIEND THE PARTRIDGE.

HERE is another instance of friendship existing between a dog and a bird.

THE SPANIEL AND HIS FRIEND THE PARTRIDGE.

A lady possessed a spaniel named Tom. After she had had Tom several years, a red-legged partridge called Bill, brought from France, was given to her. She had often seen Tom tease the cats and amuse himself with barking at birds, and was consequently afraid to place Bill near him. One day, however, Bill was brought into the room, and placed on the ground, a watch being kept on Tom's movements. Bill appeared in no way alarmed at his four-footed companion, who, too, seemed not inclined to molest him. They looked at each other shyly at first, like two children when first introduced; but Bill hopping forward, Tom seemed pleased at the confidence shown in him.

In a short time they became excellent friends. A saucer of bread and milk being placed on the ground, they fed out of it together, and afterwards would retire to a corner to sleep, the partridge nestling between the dog's legs, and never stirring till his companion awoke.

When the dog accompanied his mistress in a walk, the bird, which could not be taken, showed much uneasiness till he returned; and one day, when the partridge happened to be shut up in a room by himself, the dog searched all over the house, whining mournfully, as if he feared some accident had happened to his friend.

This curious friendship came to an untimely end. Tom was stolen; and from that time Bill refused food, and died on the seventh day, a victim to grief for the loss of his companion.

My dear young friends, let the story of this strange friendship awaken in your minds a stronger sense of love and trust, not only towards those who may be the friends of your youth, but also towards all who may have the care or oversight of you. I am afraid there are very many young persons who would display far less genuine grief at the loss of their companions than did the partridge at the loss of the spaniel. Strive, then, to let your friendship towards them be such, that your grief at their loss may be genuine.

THE DOG WHICH TRACED HIS MASTER.

Dogs often show much regard for each other, as well as for other animals; but they certainly possess a still greater affection for human beings.

A gentleman having to proceed from the north of England to London by sea, left his favourite dog behind. While seated one night in the pit of Drury Lane Theatre —some time after his arrival in the metropolis—to his amazement, his favourite sprang upon him, covering him with caresses.

The dog, as soon as he found that his master had departed from the shore, broke his chain, and set out on his long journey to rejoin him. How he traced him must ever be a marvel. Perhaps he pursued the line of coast till he reached London, where it is possible he may have recovered some trace of his lost friend by scent, at the landing place. This, however, is so improbable, that it is more likely he made the discovery by that incomprehensible power which we call instinct.

THE DOG WHICH TRAVELLED ALONE BY RAILWAY.

A PRESTON paper gave some time ago an account of a dog which travelled alone by railway in search of his master. In this instance the animal acted much as any human being would have done.

The dog, which was well known to the railway officials from frequently travelling with his master, presented himself at one of the stations on the Fleetwood, Preston, and Longridge line. After looking round for some length of time among the passengers and in the carriages, just as the train was about to start he leaped into one of the compartments of a carriage, and lay down under a seat.

Arrived at Longridge, he made another survey of the passengers, and after waiting till the station had been cleared, he went into the Railway Station Hotel, searched all the places on the ground-floor, then went and made a tour of inspection over the adjoining grounds ; but being apparently unsuccessful, trotted back to the train, and took his late position just as it was moving off. On reaching the station from which he had first started, he again looked round as before, then took his departure.

It seems that he now proceeded to the General Railway Station at Preston, and after repeating the looking-round performance, placed himself under one of the seats in a train which he had singled out of the many that are constantly popping in and out, and in due time arrived in Liverpool. He now visited a few places where he had before been with his master. He remained over-night in Liverpool, and visited Preston early again the following morning.

Still not finding his missing master, he for the fourth time took the train ; on this occasion, however, to Lancaster and Carlisle, at which latter place, his sagacity, as well as the persevering tact he had displayed in prosecuting his search, were rewarded by finding his master. Their joy at meeting was mutual.

I cannot too often repeat it : let duty be your master. Be not less persevering in pursuing it, than were the dogs I have told you about in seeking their masters.

NEPTUNE; OR, FAITHFUL TO TRUST.

AT an inn in Wimborne in Dorsetshire, near which town I resided, was kept, some years ago, a magnificent Newfoundland dog called Neptune. His fame was celebrated far and wide. Every morning he was accustomed, as the clock of the minster struck eight, to take in his mouth a basket containing a certain number of pence, and to carry it across the street to the shop of a baker, who took out the money, and replaced it by its value in rolls. With these Neptune hastened back to the kitchen, and speedily deposited his trust.

It is remarkable that he never attempted to take the basket, nor even to approach it, on Sunday mornings, when no rolls were to be obtained.

On one occasion, when returning with the rolls, another dog made an attack upon the basket, for the purpose of stealing its contents. On this the trusty fellow, placing it on the ground, severely punished his assailant, and then bore off his charge in triumph.

He met his death—with many other dogs in the place—from poison, which was scattered about the town by a semi-insane person, in revenge for some fancied insult he had received from the inhabitants.

Like trusty Neptune, deserve the confidence placed in you, by battling bravely against all temptations to act dishonestly. Your friends may never know of your efforts to do so, but your own peace of mind will be reward enough.

THE AFFECTIONATE POODLE.

A GENTLEMAN residing at Dresden possessed a poodle which he had always treated kindly, and which was especially fond of him. He at length, however, made a present of her to a friend living about nine miles off. It being supposed that she would probably try to return to her former master, she was tied up till she became the mother of three young puppies ; and so devoted to them did she appear, that her new owner no longer feared she would quit him. He therefore gave her her liberty.

Shortly afterwards, however, she and the three puppies were missing. Search was made for them in vain. At length her master's Dresden friend paid him a visit, and told him that on the preceding evening the poodle had arrived at his house with one of her puppies in her mouth, and that another had been found dead on the road.

THE AFFECTIONATE POODLE.

It appeared that she had started at night, carrying the pups—which were still too young to walk—one at a time, a certain distance, intending to go back for the others. She had hoped thus to transfer them all to her former much-loved home. The third puppy was never found. The one that died had perished by cold, it being the winter season.

THE NEWFOUNDLAND DOG AND THE HATS.

IN sagacity, the Newfoundland surpasses dogs of all other breeds.

Two gentlemen, brothers, were out shooting wild-fowl, attended by one of these noble animals. Having thrown down their hats on the grass, they together crept through some reeds to the river-bank, along which they proceeded some way, after firing at the birds. Wishing at length for their hats—one of which was smaller than the other—they sent the dog back for them. The animal, believing it was his duty to bring both together, made several attempts to carry them in his mouth. Finding some difficulty in doing this, he placed the smaller hat within the larger one, and pressed it down with his foot. He was thus, with ease, enabled to carry them both at the same time.

Perhaps he had seen old-clothes-men thus carrying hats; but I am inclined to think that he was guided by seeing that this was the best way to effect his object.

There are two ways of doing everything—a wrong and a right one. Like the Newfoundland dog, try to find out the right way, and do what you have to do, in that way.

THE NEWFOUNDLAND DOG AND THE WRECK.

How often has the noble Newfoundland dog been the means of saving the lives of those perishing in the water!

A heavy gale was blowing, when a vessel was seen driving toward the coast of Kent. She struck, and the surf rolled furiously round her. Eight human beings were observed clinging to the wreck, but no ordinary boat could be launched to their aid ; and in those days, I believe, no lifeboats existed,—at all events, not as they do now, on all parts of the coast. It was feared every moment that the unfortunate seamen would perish, when a gentleman came down to the beach, accompanied by a Newfoundland dog. He saw that, if a line could be stretched between the wreck and the shore, the people might be saved ; but it could only be carried from the vessel to the shore. He knew how it must be done.

Putting a short stick in the mouth of the animal, he pointed to the vessel. The courageous dog understood his meaning, and springing into the sea, fought his way through the waves. In vain, however, he strove to get up the vessel's side ; but he was seen by the crew, who, making fast a rope to another piece of wood, hove it toward him. The sagacious animal understood the object, and seizing the piece of wood, dragged it through the surf, and delivered it to his master. A line of communication was thus formed between the vessel and the shore, and every man on board was rescued from a watery grave.

DANDIE, THE MISER.

DANDIE, a Newfoundland dog belonging to Mr. M'Intyre of Edinburgh, stands unrivalled for his cleverness and the peculiarity of his habits. Dandie would bring any article he was sent for by his master, selecting it from a heap of others of the same description.

One evening, when a party was assembled, one of them dropped a shilling. After a diligent search, it could nowhere be found. Mr. M'Intyre then called to Dandie, who had been crouching in a corner of the room, and said to him, "Find the shilling, Dandie, and you shall have a biscuit." On this Dandie rose, and placed the coin, which he had picked up unperceived by those present, upon the table.

Dandie, who had many friends, was accustomed to receive a penny from them every day, which he took to a baker's and exchanged for a loaf of bread for himself. It happened that one of them was accosted by Dandie for his usual present, when he had no money in his pocket. "I have not a penny with me to-day, but I have one at home," said the gentleman, scarcely believing that Dandie understood him. On returning to his house, however, he met Dandie at the door, demanding admittance, evidently come for his penny. The gentleman, happening to have a bad penny, gave it him; but the baker refused to give him a loaf for it. Dandie, receiving it back, returned to the door of the donor, and when a servant had opened it, laid the false coin at her feet, and walked away with an indignant air.

Dandie, however, frequently received more money than

DANDIE. THE MISER.

he required for his necessities, and took to hoarding it up. This was discovered by his master, in consequence of his appearing one Sunday morning with a loaf in his mouth, when it was not likely he would have received a present. Suspecting this, Mr. M'Intyre told a servant to search his room—in which Dandie slept—for money. The dog watched her, apparently unconcerned, till she approached his bed, when, seizing her gown, he drew her from it. On her persisting, he growled, and struggled so violently that his master was obliged to hold him, when the woman discovered sevenpence-halfpenny. From that time forward he exhibited a strong dislike to the woman, and used to hide his money under a heap of dust at the back of the premises.

People thought Dandie a very clever dog—as he was— but there are many things far better than cleverness. It strikes me that he was a very selfish fellow, and therefore, like selfish boys and girls, unamiable. He was an arrant beggar too. I'll say no more about him. Pray do not imitate Dandie.

THE DOG AND THE BURGLAR.

SOME years ago, a stranger arrived at the house of a shopkeeper in Deptford who let lodgings, stating that he had just arrived from the West Indies, and would take possession of rooms the next day, but would send his trunk that night. The trunk was brought late in the evening by two porters, who were desired, as it was heavy, to carry it to the bedroom.

As soon as the family had retired to rest, a little spaniel.

which usually slept in the shop, made his way to the door of the chamber where the chest was deposited, and putting his nose close to it, began to bark furiously. The people, thus aroused, opened the door, when the dog flew towards the trunk, and barked and scratched against it with the greatest vehemence. In vain they attempted to draw him away. A neighbour was called in, when, on moving the trunk, it was suspected that it must contain something alive. They accordingly forced it open, when out came the new lodger; who had caused himself to be thus brought into the house for the purpose of robbing it.

If you let lodgings in your heart to strangers, take care that your little spaniel Conscience keeps wide awake, lest some evening a chest may be brought in containing a thief who may rob you before you find out his character. The thief may be an evil thought, a bad feeling, shut up in a chest formed of self-indulgence, sloth, vanity, pride. At the first alarm, wake up, break open the chest, call in your faithful neighbour, and hand over the new lodger to justice.

THE POODLE AND THE STRANGER ROBBER.

AN English gentleman travelling abroad was accompanied by a favourite poodle. On one occasion he met an agreeable stranger at an hotel, to whom, as they were both going the same way, he offered a seat in his carriage. No sooner, however, had the stranger entered the vehicle than the poodle, which had from the first shown a dislike to the man, manifested even a greater aversion to him than before.

They put up for the night at a small inn in a wild and
little frequented country ; and on separating to go to their
respective rooms, the poodle again snarled at the stranger,
and was with difficulty restrained from biting him.

The Englishman was awakened in the middle of the
night by a noise in his room, into which the moonbeams
streamed, and there he saw the dog struggling with his
travelling companion.   On being overpowered, the stranger
confessed that he had come for the purpose of stealing the
traveller's money, being aware that he had a considerable
sum with him.

You have not the instinct which has been given to some
dogs, and which enables them, for their master's protection,
to detect persons harbouring evil intentions towards them;
but when you meet with a boy or man careless in his conversation, a swearer, or expressing irreligious or immoral
opinions, however courteous and agreeable he may otherwise be, do not associate with him a moment longer than
you can help, or he will rob you of what is of far more
value than a purse of gold.

THE DOG HOLDING THE THIEF.

A DOG of the Highland breed, belonging to Lord Arbuth-
not, treated a thief in much the same way as my friend's
dog did the robber of his apple-orchard.

The servants, going out one morning, found a man lying
on the ground, a short way from the stable, with a number
of bridles and other horse-trappings near him, and the dog

holding him by the trousers. Directly the servants appeared the dog let go his hold, when the man confessed that the dog had thus held him for five hours.

When a bad thought or desire steals into your heart, or, properly speaking, rises in it, hold it down, as the dog did the thief, till you are able to rid yourself of it.

THE FAITHLESS WATCH-DOG.

FAITHFUL as dogs are in general, I am sorry to have to record an instance to the contrary.

A watch-dog, whose special duty was to remain at his post during the night, found that his collar was sufficiently loose to allow him to withdraw his head from it whenever he pleased. He acted as some human beings do whose right principles do not fit tightly to their necks—slipping out of them at the very time they ought to keep them on. The dog was, however, sagacious enough to know that if he did so during the day he would be seen by his master, when to a certainty the collar would be tightened. But no sooner did night arrive, and the lights began to disappear from the windows, than he used to slip his head out of his collar, and roam about the neighbouring fields, sometimes picking up a hare or rabbit for his supper.

Knowing also that the blood on his mouth would betray him, he would, after his banquet, go to a stream and wash it off. This done, he would return before daybreak to his kennel, and slipping his head into his collar, lie down in his bed, as though he had remained there on the watch all the night.

Now I must beg my young readers to remember, should they be tempted to do what is wrong, that however well-behaved they may contrive to appear before their friends and acquaintances, in their own mind there will always be the unpleasant feeling arising from the consciousness of doing a guilty action.

THE SHOEBLACK'S DOG.

Dogs have been frequently trained to act roguish parts.

An English officer visiting Paris, was annoyed one day by having a little poodle run up to him and rub his muddy paws over his boots. Near at hand was seated a shoeblack, to whom he went to have his boots repolished. Having been annoyed in a similar manner by the same dog, several times in succession, he watched the animal, when he observed him dip his paws in the mud on the banks of the Seine, and then go and rub them on the boots of the best-dressed people passing at the time.

Discovering at length that the dog belonged to the shoeblack, the gentleman questioned the man, who confessed that he had taught the dog the trick in order to bring business to himself. "And will you part with your clever dog?" asked the gentleman. The shoeblack consented, and a price was fixed upon and paid. The dog accompanied his new master to London, and was shut up for some time, till it was believed that he would remain con-

THE FAITHLESS WATCH-DOG

tentedly in the house. No sooner, however, did he obtain his liberty, than he decamped; and a fortnight afterwards he was found with his former master, pursuing his old occupation.

This story shows the difficulty of getting rid of bad habits, and proves that as dogs have been trained, so will they—as well as children—continue to act. The poor poodle, however, knew no better. He was faithful to his former master, and thought that he was doing his duty. But boys and girls do know perfectly well when they are acting rightly or wrongly, and should strive unceasingly to overcome their bad habits.

THE TERRIER AND THE PIN.

A TERRIER—deservedly a pet in the family for his gentleness and amiability—was playing with one of the children, when suddenly he was heard to utter a snarl, followed by a bark. The mother rushed to her child, and believing it to have been bitten, drove off the dog. No injury, however, was apparent. The dog retired to a corner, where he remained, in an attitude of regret, till the inspection had been finished. He then approached the lady, and with a touch of his paw claimed attention. It was given, and forthwith he deposited at her feet a pin.

The story was thus made plain. The child, finding the pin, had turned the dog's nose into a pin-cushion. The snarl rebuked the offence, and the pin had been taken by the dog, with his mouth, out of the child's hand. No sooner did the dog see that this was understood, than he began to lick the little fellow's hand, as if to assure him of his forgiveness, and to beg him to make friends again,—which they were ever afterwards.

I hope that the little boy, through his whole life, was always ready to profit by the lesson of his dumb companion and to forgive injuries.

THE DOG AND HIS INJURED FRIEND.

DOGS frequently form warm friendships, and help each other in time of trouble.

Two dogs belonging to the same owner had become great friends. Ponto and Dick, we will call them, though I am not quite certain as to their names. Ponto's leg being broken, he was kept a close prisoner. His friend Dick, instead of whining out a few commonplace expressions of sympathy,—"Dear me, I'm so sorry; well, I hope you will soon get better," and then scampering off to amuse himself with other dogs in the village, or to run after the cows, or to go out hunting,—came and sat down by his side, showing him every mark of attention. Then, after a time, Dick started up, exclaiming,—"Ponto, I am sure you must be hungry; it is dull work for you lying there with nothing to do." Without waiting for Ponto to beg that he would not trouble himself, off he set, and soon brought back a nice bone with plenty of gristle on it. "There, old fellow, munch away—it will amuse you," he remarked, putting his prize down under his friend's nose.

After watching complacently as poor Ponto gnawed away with somewhat languid jaws, till the bone was scraped almost clean, he again set out in search of another. After he had brought in several, he lay down as before by his friend's side, just playing with one of the bones to keep him company. Thus day after day Dick continued to cheer and comfort his injured friend with unfailing constancy till he completely recovered.

When dogs thus exhibit disinterested kindness and self-sacrifice, how ought human beings to behave to those suffering from pain or sorrow? When tempted to run off and amuse yourself, leaving a sick friend at home, remember these two dogs. Think of how much suffering there is in the world, and what room there is for kindness and compassion; and can you then be hard-hearted, or indifferent to the sufferings of others?

THE DOG AND THE SURGEON.

I MUST tell you of another dog which showed not only affection for a companion, but a wonderful amount of sense. He once broke his leg, in which state he was found by a kind surgeon, who took him home, set his leg, and after he had recovered allowed him to go away. The dog did not forget the treatment he had received, nor the person from whom he had received it.

Some months afterwards, he found another dog to whom the same accident had happened. By the language which dogs employ, he told his friend all about his own cure, and,

THE DOG AND HIS INJURED FRIEND.

assisting him along the road, led him, late at night, to the surgeon's house. He there barked loudly at the door. No one came, so he barked louder and louder. At last a window was opened, and a person looked out, whom he at once recognized ; and great was his joy when the kind surgeon, coming down-stairs, opened the door. Wagging his tail, he made such signs as he was capable of using, to show what he wanted. The surgeon soon saw what had happened to his old patient's friend, whom he took in and treated in the same skilful way. His former patient, satisfied that all was right, then ran off to attend to his proper duties.

Let us, from this kind dog's behaviour, learn, whenever we receive a benefit, to endeavour, if possible, to impart it to others, and not to remain selfishly satisfied with the advantage we ourselves have gained.

THE DOG PREVENTING THE CAT STEALING.

THE owner of a spaniel was one day called away from his dinner-table, leaving a dog and a favourite cat in the room. On his return he found the spaniel stretched her whole length along the table, by the side of a leg of mutton, while Puss was skulking in a corner. He soon saw that, though the mutton was untouched, the cat had been driven from the table by the spaniel, in the act of attempting a robbery on the meat, and that the dog had taken up his post to prevent a repetition of the attempt.

The little animal was thus in the habit of guarding eatables which she believed were left in her charge ; and while she would not touch them herself, she kept other dogs and cats at a distance.

How much evil might be prevented, if boys and girls would always act the part of the faithful little spaniel ; only, as they have got tongues in their head, and know how wrong it is to do what is bad, they can remonstrate lovingly with their companions who may be about to do a wrong thing—and then, if this fails, do their utmost to prevent them.

ONE DOG GETTING ASSISTANCE FROM ANOTHER.

Two dogs living in the neighbourhood of Cupar, in Fife, used to fight desperately whenever they met,—the one belonging to Captain R——, the other to a farmer.

Captain R——'s dog was accustomed to go on messages, and even to bring meat and other articles from Cupar in a basket. One day, while returning with a supply of mutton, he was attacked by a number of curs in the town, eager to obtain the tempting prize. The messenger fought bravely, but at length, overpowered, was compelled to yield up the basket, though not before he had secured some of the meat. With this he hastened at full speed to the quarters of his enemy, at whose feet he laid it down, stretching himself beside him till he had eaten it up. A few sniffs, a few whispers in the ear, and other dog-like courtesies were then exchanged, after which they both set out together for Cupar, where they worried almost every dog in the town, and, returning home, were ever afterwards on the most friendly terms.

Remember that there are no human beings whose conduct at all times it is safe to follow.

Revenge is wrong, but let us ever be ready to help and defend those who are ill-treated and oppressed.

THE POINTER AND THE BAD SHOT.

Dogs, like human beings, show that they can criticise the conduct of those they serve.

A gentleman from London, more accustomed to handle an umbrella than a gun, went down to the house of a friend in the country to enjoy a day's shooting.

" You shall have one of my best pointers," said his friend, "but recollect, he will stand no nonsense. If you kill the birds, well and good ; if not, I cannot answer for the consequences."

The would-be sportsman shouldered his gun and marched off. As he traversed the fields, the pointer, ranging before him, marked bird after bird, which were as often missed. The pointer looked back, evidently annoyed, and after this frequently ran over game. At length he made a dead stop near a low bush, with his nose pointed downwards, his forefeet bent, his tail straight and steady. The gentleman approached with both barrels cocked. Again the dog moved steadily forward a few paces, expressing the anxiety of his mind by moving his tail backwards and forwards. At length a brace of partridges slowly rose. Who could possibly miss them ! Bang ! bang ! went both barrels,

THE POINTER AND THE BAD SHOT

but the birds continued their flight unharmed. The dog now fairly lost patience, turned round, placed his tail between his legs, gave one sad howl, long and loud, and set off at full speed homeward, leaving the gentleman to holloa after him at the top of a gate, and continue the shooting as best he could by himself.

If you desire to be properly served by those you employ, you must be up to your business. I have often heard young people complain that they can do nothing properly, the servants are so stupid; when they come down late, that they were not called in time ; or, if they have not learned their lessons, that the room was not ready. I daresay, when the Cockney sportsman returned with an empty game-bag, he abused the stupid dog for running away.

BASS, THE GREAT ST. BERNARD DOG.

SIR THOMAS DICK LAUDER had a dog named Bass, brought when a puppy from the Great St. Bernard. His bark was tremendous, and might be distinguished nearly a mile off.

He was once stolen, when a letter-carrier, well acquainted with him, heard his bark from the inside of a yard, and insisted on the man who had him in possession delivering him up.

Terrific as was his bark, he was so good-natured that he would never fight other dogs ; and even allowed a little King Charles spaniel named Raith to run off with any bone he might have been gnawing, and to tyrannize over him in a variety of ways. If attacked by an inferior enemy, he would throw his immense bulk down upon his anta-gonist and nearly smother him, without attempting to bite.

He took a particular fancy for one of the Edinburgh postmen, whose duty it was, besides delivering letters, to carry a letter-bag from one receiving-house to another. This bag he used to give Bass to carry. The dog accom-panied him on his rounds, but invariably parted with him opposite the gate of the Convent of St. Margaret, and returned home.

On one occasion the postman, being ill, sent another man in his place. Bass went up to the stranger, who naturally retired before so formidable-looking a dog. Bass followed, showing a determination to have the post-bag. The man did all he could to keep possession of it; but at length Bass, seeing that it was not likely to be given to him, raised him-self on his hind-legs, and putting a great fore-paw on each of the man's shoulders, laid him flat on his back in the road, then quietly picking up the bag, proceeded peaceably on his wonted way. The man followed, ineffectually attempting to coax the dog to give up the bag. At the first house at which he arrived, the people comforted him by telling him that the dog always carried the bag. Bass walked with the man to all the houses at which he delivered letters, and along the road, till he came to the gate of St. Margaret's, where he dropped the bag and returned home.

Accounts exist of the services rendered by these noble dogs of St. Bernard in saving life among the snowy regions of the Alps. It is recounted that one of these dogs pre-served twenty-two lives. He at length lost his own in an avalanche, when those he was endeavouring to assist also perished.

THE DOG AND THE NEWSPAPER.

SEVERAL dogs have been taught to go to the post-office for their masters' newspapers, or to receive them from the newsman.

A neighbour of mine, who was fond of telling good stories—which he did not always, perhaps, expect his guests to believe—used to give an account of the cleverness of one of his dogs. The dog went regularly every morning into the neighbouring town for the *Times*, and brought it back before breakfast. This was a fact.

On one occasion the dog returned without a paper,—so my neighbour used to tell the story. His master sent him back again, when he once more appeared with no paper in his mouth. On this the owner ordered his cob, and rode into the town to inquire of the postmaster why the paper had not come. "Sir," answered the postmaster, "your *Times* did not arrive this morning; but when I offered the dog the *Morning Post* he refused to receive it."

THE STEADY POINTER.

IT is wonderful how completely dogs can be trained to the performance of their duties.

A well-practised pointer was about to leap over a rail, when she perceived a nest of partridges close to her nose.

THE STEADY POINTER.

Had she moved an inch she would have frightened them away. There she stood for more than two hours, with her legs on the upper bar, awaiting the arrival of the sportsman. For some time she was not discovered, and not till he appeared would she quit her post, when, the birds rising, some of them were shot; but the steady pointer was so stiff when thus relieved that she could scarcely move.

Here is an example which my young readers should endeavour to follow when they have a duty, however irksome, to perform. Remain steadily at your post; let nothing draw you away. Do not say, I have stopped at work long enough, I am sick of it. When tempted to give up, remember THE STEADY POINTER.

THE YOUNG DOCTOR AND PINCHER.

ONE of the cleverest and most amusing of dogs was Pincher, a rough Scotch terrier, belonging to Mrs. Lee's brother.* The boy had a great fancy to be a doctor. Having manufactured a variety of surgical instruments out of flint stones, he pretended to perform with them operations on Pincher, who would lie perfectly still while his teeth were drawn, his limbs set, his veins opened, or his wounds bandaged.

The pretended doctor, finally copying the process practised on pigs, used to cut up his favourite entirely. The dog was laid on the table, when he stuck out his legs as stiffly as possible. Preparations were first made for cutting off his head; and immediately the flint was passed across

Mrs. Lee's " Anecdotes of Animals."

the throat it fell on one side, and remained so completely without motion that it might have been thought the dog fancied it was really off. Each leg in succession was then operated on, and as the instrument passed round them the dog made them fall, putting them as close as possible to the body. When the operation was concluded, the boy used to exclaim, "Jump up, good dog;" and Pincher, bounding off the table, would shake himself to life again.

SIRRAH, THE ETTRICK SHEPHERD'S DOG.

SIRRAH, fortunately for his fame, possessed a master in James Hogg, the Ettrick Shepherd, well able to recount his history. Hogg bought Sirrah of a drover for a guinea, observing, notwithstanding his dejected and forlorn appearance, a sort of sullen intelligence in his countenance. Though he had never turned a sheep in his life, as soon as he discovered it was his duty to do so he began with eagerness and anxiety to learn his evolutions. He would try every way deliberately till he found out what his master wanted him to do; and when once he understood a direction he never forgot it again or mistook it.

Often, when hard pressed in accomplishing a task he was put to, he had expedients for the moment that bespoke a great share of the reasoning faculty. On one occasion about seven hundred lambs which were under Hogg's care at weaning-time broke up at midnight, and scampered off in three divisions across the neighbouring hills, in spite of all he and an assistant could do to keep them together. The night was so dark that Sirrah could not be seen, but the faithful animal had heard his master lament their absence in words which set him at once on the alert, and without more ado he had silently gone off in quest of the recreant flock. In vain Hogg and his assistant spent the whole night in searching for their lost charge; and they were on their way home to inform their master of their loss, when they discovered a lot of lambs at the bottom of a deep ravine, and the indefatigable Sirrah standing in front of them, looking round for some relief, but still true to his charge. Believing that it was one only of the divisions, what was their astonishment when they discovered the whole flock, and not one lamb awanting! How he had got all the divisions collected in the dark it is impossible to say. The charge was left to him from midnight till the rising sun, and if all the shepherds in the forest had been there to assist him they could not have effected it with greater propriety.

Hogg relates many other anecdotes of Sirrah. On one occasion he brought back a wild ewe which no one could catch from amid numerous flocks of sheep. He showed great indignation when the ewe, being brought home, was set at liberty among the other sheep of his master. He had understood that the animal was to be kept by itself, and that he was to be the instrument of keeping it so, and he considered himself insulted by the ewe being allowed to go among other sheep, after he had been required to make such exertion, and had made it so successfully, to keep it separate.

A single shepherd and his dog, says Hogg, will accom-plish more in collecting Highland sheep from a farm than twenty shepherds could do without dogs. Without the shepherd's dog, the whole of the mountainous land in Scotland would not be worth sixpence. It would require more hands to gather a flock of sheep from the hills into their folds, and drive them to market, than the profits of the whole flock would be capable of maintaining.

Here we have an example of a dull, unattractive-looking dog becoming of the very utmost canine usefulness. I have known many an apparently dull boy, by perseveringly endeavouring to learn what he has had to do, and then steadily pursuing the course marked out for him, rise far above his quick and so-called clever but careless companions. I do not say, Work for the purpose of rising, but, Work because it is right. Remember Sirrah. Learn your duty, and do it, however disagreeable it may seem.

THE DOG AND THE FOWLS.

A HOUSE-DOG, whose kennel was in a farm-yard, used to have his mess of food brought to him daily in a tin can, and placed before his abode. No sooner had the cook disappeared, than the poultry were in the habit of collecting round and abstracting the contents of the can. The dog—a good-natured animal—bore their pilfering for some time without complaining; but at length, as they carried off more than he considered fair, he warned them away, by growling and exhibiting his teeth. Notwithstanding this they again returned to the can, when the dog, instead of seizing some of his persecutors, lifted the can in his mouth,

and conveyed it within his kennel, where he finished his
meal in peace, while the cocks and hens stood watching
without, afraid to enter.

Depend on it, you will often find the means of avoiding
annoyances much after the method pursued by that sensible
house-dog, without retaliating on those who annoy you. If
you cannot otherwise pacify them, remove the cause of dis-
pute out of sight.

BARBEKARK, THE GREENLAND DOG.

THE dog is the companion of the savage, as well as the
civilized man, in all parts of the world. He accompanies
the wretched Fuegan in his hunts, partaking somewhat of
the character of his master ; and is the friend and assistant
of the Esquimaux in the Arctic regions. The Esquimaux
dogs, though hardly treated, show great affection for their
masters, and frequently exhibit much sagacity.

Captain Hall, the Arctic explorer, had a Greenland dog
called Barbekark. One day they were out hunting on the
frozen, snow-covered sea, when a herd of deer appeared in
sight. Chase was given. One was wounded, but not
killed, and off went the herd as fleet as the wind, now
turning in one direction, now in another, among the ice-
hummocks. The rest of the dogs followed in their tracks.
Barbekark, however, was seen to strike away in a direct
line over the snow, regardless of the animals' footsteps.
On and on went Barbekark, straight for a spot which
brought him close upon the deer. The latter immediately
changed their course, and so did Barbekark, hot in pursuit

THE DOG AND THE FOWLS.

of them.   At length the hunters, unable longer to endure
the cold, were compelled to return to the ship, believing
that the deer had escaped.

At mid-day Barbekark appeared on board, with blood
round his mouth and over his body.   It was supposed that
he had fallen in with the deer, but not that he could
possibly have killed one.   He, however, showed by his
actions that he wished to draw the attention of the crew
to the quarter where he had been chasing.   He kept
whining, going first to one, then to another, now running
towards the gangway steps, then back again.   At last, one
of the men having to visit the wreck of a vessel which lay
near, Barbekark followed; but seeing that the man went no
further, off went Barbekark to the north-west by himself.
On this, some of the crew, convinced that he must have
killed a deer, put on their thick coats and followed him.
They proceeded nearly three miles, when they found
Barbekark and the other Greenland dogs seated upon their
haunches round a deer lying dead before them.   The throat
of the poor animal had been cut with Barbekark's teeth as
effectually as by the knife of a white man or Esquimaux,
and a piece of the tongue had been bitten out.

As soon as the sailors appeared, Barbekark jumped from
his watchful position, and ran to meet them with manifes-
tations of delight, looking up at them, as much as to say:
"I have done the best I could; I have killed the deer, and
eaten just one luscious mouthful.   And now I give up the
animal to you, and merely ask for myself and companions,
who have been faithfully guarding the prize, such portion as
you yourselves may disdain."   Several crows were pecking

away at the carcass, but Barbekark and they were always on good terms. Sometimes, indeed, he allowed them to rest upon his back; and consequently he did not drive them away.

On another occasion a party of the explorers were out with a sleigh and dogs, and among them was Barbekark. They were caught in a fearful gale, the snow beating in their faces. Esquimaux dogs are often unmanageable when an attempt is made to force them in the teeth of a storm; and so it now proved. The leader lost his way and confused the rest. The men as well as the dogs were becoming blinded. The leading dog directed the team towards some islands; but on approaching them it was seen that Barbekark was struggling to make a different route. Happily, he was allowed to have his own way, and in a short time he led the party direct to the ship.

THE ESQUIMAUX DOG SMILE.

CAPTAIN HALL had another dog, Smile by name, the noblest looking, the best leader, and seal and bear dog, ever met with. One day he was out with dogs and sleigh where the ice was still firm, when suddenly a seal was noticed ahead. In an instant the dogs were dashing towards the prey, drawing the sledge after them at a marvellous rate, led by Smile. The seal for a moment seemed frightened, and kept on the ice a second or two too long; for just as he plunged, Smile caught him by the tail and flippers. The seal struggled violently, and so did Smile, making the sledge caper about

merrily; but in a moment more the other dogs laid hold,
and aided in dragging the seal out of his hole on to the
ice, when Smile took it in charge. The prize was
secured entirely by the dogs, indeed, without any aid from
the men.

CHAPTER III.

Horses.

THE MARE AND HER FOAL.

THE horse becomes the willing servant of man, and when kindly treated looks upon him as a friend and protector.

I have an interesting story to tell you of a mare which belonged to Captain I——, an old settler in New Zealand. She and her foal had been placed in a paddock, between which and her master's residence, three or four miles away, several high fences intervened. The paddock itself was surrounded by a still higher fence.

One day, however, as Captain I—— was standing with a friend in front of his house, he was surprised to see the mare come galloping up. Supposing that the fence of her paddock had been broken down, and that, pleased at finding herself at liberty, she had leaped the others, he ordered a servant to take her back. The mare willingly followed the man; but in a short time was seen galloping up towards the house in as great a hurry as before. The servant, who arrived some time afterwards, assured his master that he

had put the mare safely into the paddock.   Captain I——
told him again to take back the animal, and to examine the
fence more thoroughly, still believing that it must have
been broken down in some part or other, though the gate
might be secure.

Captain I—— and his friend then retired into the house,
and were seated at dinner, when the sound of horse's hoofs
reached their ears.   The friend, who had on this got up to
look out of the window, saw that it was the mare come
back for the third time; and observing the remarkable
manner in which she was running up and down, apparently
trying even to get into the house, exclaimed, "What can
that mare want?   I am sure that there is something the
matter."   Captain I—— on hearing this hurried out to
ascertain the state of the case.   No sooner did the mare
see him than she began to frisk about and exhibit the most
lively satisfaction; but instead of stopping to receive the
accustomed caress, off she set again of her own accord
towards the paddock, looking back to ascertain whether
her master was following.   His friend now joined him, and
the mare, finding that they were keeping close behind her,
trotted on till the gate of the paddock was reached, where
she waited for them.   On its being opened, she led them
across the field to a deep ditch on the farther side, when,
what was their surprise to find that her colt had fallen into
it, and was struggling on its back with its legs in the air,
utterly unable to extricate itself.   In a few minutes more
probably it would have been dead.   The mare, it was
evident, finding that the servant did not comprehend her
wishes, had again and again sought her master, in whom

she had learned from past experience to confide. Here was an example of strong maternal affection eliciting a faculty superior to instinct, which fully merits the name of reason.

The aid of a kind master will always be sought in time of need. The conduct of the mare speaks much in favour of her owner. It is evident that he treated her well. Had such not been the case, it is not at all likely that the animal would have persisted in coming direct to him in her time of need. Be ready, then, to fly for succour to those about you whom you may have found willing to help and serve you.

THE NEWSMAN'S HORSE.

THE memory of horses is most remarkable. The newsman of a provincial paper was in the habit of riding his horse once or twice a week to the houses of fifty or sixty of his customers, the horse invariably stopping of his own accord at each house as he reached it.

But the memory of the horse was exhibited in a still more curious manner. It happened that there were two persons on the route who took one paper between them, and each claimed the privilege of having it first on each alternate week. The horse soon became accustomed to this regulation, and though the parties lived two miles distant, he stopped once a fortnight at the door of the half-customer at one place, and once a fortnight at the door of the half-customer at the other; and never did he forget this arrangement, which lasted for several years.

If an animal can thus become so regular in his habits,

and remember his duty so well as did this newsman's horse, surely you, my readers, whether young or old, have no excuse when you forget yours, and neglect to be at the appointed place at the proper time.

THE TWO WISE CART-HORSES.

CART-HORSES, though heavy-looking animals, are more sagacious that their more gracefully formed relatives.

A cart-horse had been driven from a farm-yard to the neighbouring brook early one morning during winter to drink. The water was frozen over, and the horse stamped away with his fore-feet, but was unable to break the ice. Finding this, he waited till a companion came down, when the two, standing side by side, and causing their hoofs to descend together, broke through the ice, and were thus enabled to obtain the water they required.

What one person alone cannot do, two working heartily together may accomplish. We shall find no lack of thick ice to break through. The thickest, perhaps, is the icy opposition of cold, stubborn hearts to what is right and good. Let us beware that our hearts do not freeze, but take care to keep them warm by exercising them in the service of love and kindness.

THE TWO WISE CART-HORSES.

THE AUTHOR'S HORSE BECOMING HIS GUIDE.

I WAS once travelling in the interior of Portugal with several companions. My horse had never been in that part of the country before. We left our inn at daybreak, and proceeded through a mountainous district to visit some beautiful scenery. On our return evening was approaching, when I stopped behind my companions to tighten the girths of my saddle. Believing that there was only one path to take, I rode slowly on, but shortly reached a spot where I was in some doubt whether I should go forward or turn off to the left. I shouted, but heard no voice in reply, nor could I see any trace of my friends. Darkness was coming rapidly on. My horse seeming inclined to take the left hand, I thought it best to let him do so. In a short time the sky became overcast, and there was no moon. The darkness was excessive. Still my steed stepped boldly on. So dense became the obscurity, that I could not see his ears; nor could I, indeed, distinguish my own hand held out at arm's-length. I had no help for it but to place the reins on my horse's neck and let him go forward.

We had heard of robberies and murders committed; and I knew that there were steep precipices, down which, had my horse fallen, we should have been dashed to pieces. Still the firm way in which he trotted gave me confidence. Hour after hour passed by. The darkness would, at all events, conceal me from the banditti, if such were in wait —that was one consolation; but then I could not tell where my horse might be taking me. It might be far away from where I hoped to find my companions.

At length I heard a dog bark, and saw a light twinkling far down beneath me, by which I knew that I was still on the mountain-side. Thus on my steady steed proceeded, till I found that he was going along a road, and I fancied I could distinguish the outlines of trees on either hand. Suddenly he turned on one side, when my hat was nearly knocked off by striking against the beam of a trellised porch, covered with vines; and to my joy I found that he had brought me up to the door of the inn which we had left in the morning.

My companions, trusting to their human guide, had not arrived, having taken a longer though safer route. My steed had followed the direct path over the mountains which we had pursued in the morning.

Another horse of mine, which always appeared a gentle animal, and which constantly carried a lady, was, during my absence, ridden by a friend with spurs. On my return, I found that he had on several occasions attacked his rider, when dismounted, with his fore-feet, and had once carried off the rim of his hat. From that time forward he would allow no one to approach him if he saw spurs on his heels; and I was obliged to blindfold him when mounting and dismounting, as he on several occasions attacked me as he had done my friend.

My horse had till that time been a willing, quiet animal. How many human beings have, by thoughtless, cruel treatment, been turned from faithful servants into implacable foes. I must urge my young readers always to treat those who may be dependent on them with kindness and gentleness, rather because it is their duty so to do, than from fear of the consequences of an opposite course.

THE WISE HORSE AND THE PUMP.

A HORSE was shut up in a paddock near Leeds, in a corner of which stood a pump with a tub beneath it. The groom, however, often forgot to fill the tub, the horse having thus no water to drink. The animal had observed the way in which water was procured, and one night, when the tub was empty, was seen to take the pump handle in his mouth, and work it with his head till he had procured as much water as he required.

What a wise horse he was! How much wiser than some young ladies and gentlemen, who, when there is no water in their jugs, or their shoes are not cleaned, dress without washing rather than take the trouble of getting it for themselves, or wear dirty shoes rather than take them down to be cleaned, or clean them for themselves.

My young friends, remember through life that sensible horse. Take the pump by the handle, and work away with it till you have brought up the water.

THE PONY WHICH SAVED A LITTLE GIRL'S LIFE.

A SMALL pony, belonging to a gentleman in Warwickshire, was fed in a park through which a canal passes. It was

THE WISE HORSE AND THE PUMP.

a great favourite, having been long kept in the family, and was ridden by the children.

A little girl—the daughter of the owner of the property—had run out by herself into the park, and made her way to the banks of the canal. As she was playing thoughtlessly near the water, she fell in. Her cries attracted the pony, which, galloping forward, plunged into the water, and lifting her in his mouth, brought her safely to the shore.

However weak or apparently inadequate your means, you may often, if you employ them to the best of your power, render essential service to your fellow-creatures.

THE HORSE AND THE SHIPWRECK.

A REMARKABLE instance of a horse saving human life occurred some years ago at the Cape of Good Hope. A storm was raging, when a vessel, dragging her anchors, was driven on the rocks, and speedily dashed to pieces. Many of those on board perished. The remainder were seen clinging to the wreck, or holding on to the fragments which were washing to and fro amid the breakers. No boat could put off. When all hope had gone of saving the unfortunate people, a settler, somewhat advanced in life, appeared on horseback on the shore. His horse was a bold and strong animal, and noted for excelling as a swimmer. The farmer, moved with compassion for the unfortunate seamen, resolved to attempt saving them. Fixing himself firmly in the saddle, he pushed into the midst of the breakers. At first both horse and rider disappeared; but soon they were seen buffeting the waves, and swimming towards the wreck. Calling two of the seamen, he told them to hold on by his boots; then turning his horse's head, he brought them safely to land.

No less than seven times did he repeat this dangerous exploit, thus saving fourteen lives. For the eighth time he plunged in, when, encountering a formidable wave, the brave man lost his balance, and was instantly overwhelmed. The horse swam safely to shore; but his gallant rider, alas! was no more.

It is sinful uselessly to run even a slight risk of losing life; but when, on any occasion, need arises for saving the lives of our fellow-creatures, we should be willing to dare the greatest dangers in making such an effort. The fate of the brave farmer must not deter us—nor should any failure of others—from doing what is only our duty.

THE IRISH HORSE AND THE INFANT.

MRS. F—— mentions several instances of the sagacity of horses. Some horses in the county of Limerick, which were pastured in a field, broke bounds like a band of unruly schoolboys, and scrambling through a gap which they had made in a fence, found themselves in a narrow lane. Along the quiet by-road they galloped helter-skelter, at full speed, snorting and tossing their manes in the full enjoyment of their freedom, but greatly to the terror of a party of children who were playing in the lane. As the horses were seen tearing wildly along, the children scrambled up the bank into the hedge, and buried themselves in the bushes, regardless of thorns,—with the exception of one poor little thing, who, too small to run, fell down on its face, and lay crying loudly in the middle of the narrow way.

On swept the horses; but when the leader of the troop saw the little child lying in his path, he suddenly stopped, and so did the others behind him. Then stooping his head, he seized the infant's clothes with his teeth, and carefully lifted it to the side of the road, laying it gently and quite unhurt on the tender grass. He and his companions then resumed their gallop in the lane, unconscious of having performed a remarkable act.

Learn a lesson from those wild Irish horses. As you hurry along in the joyousness of youth, reflect and look before you to see whether there lies not on your road some one who requires your help. Believe me, in your path through life you will find many poor little infants who require to be lifted up and placed in safety. Do not be less obedient to the promptings of duty than were those dumb animals to the reason or the instinct implanted in their breasts.

THE HUMANE CART-HORSE AND THE CHILD.

A CARTER in Strathmiglo, Fifeshire, had an old horse, which was as familiar with his family as a dog could have been. He used to play with the children, and when they were running about between his legs he would never move, for fear of doing them an injury.

On one occasion, when dragging a loaded cart through a

THE HUMANE CART-HORSE AND THE CHILD.

narrow lane near the village, a young child, not one of his owner's family, happened to be playing on the road, and thoughtlessly ran directly before him, when, had it not been for his sagacity, it would inevitably have been crushed by the wheels. On seeing what had occurred, the good old horse took the child up by its clothes with his teeth, carried it a few yards, and then placed it by the way-side,—moving slowly all the while, and looking back occasionally, as if to satisfy himself that the cart-wheels had passed clear of it.

In all his duties he was equally steady and precise, and could be perfectly trusted.

That is just the character you should aim at deserving. To merit being perfectly trusted, shows that your talent is employed to the best advantage—that you are labouring, really and truly, from a conscious sense of duty. Only thus will you labour honestly.

THE FAITHFUL HORSE AND HIS RIDER.

HORSES have been known to fight for their friends, both human and canine.

A farmer near Edinburgh possessed a hunter which had carried him safely for many a day over moorland heath as well as beaten roads. He was one day returning from the city, where he had attended a jovial meeting, when, feeling more than usually drowsy, he slipped from his saddle to the ground, without being awakened by the change of position, and letting go the bridle as he fell. His faith-

THE FAITHFUL HORSE AND HIS RIDER.

ful steed, which had the character of being a vicious horse, instead of galloping home, as might have been expected, stood by his prostrate master, keeping as strict a watch over him as a dog could have done.

Some labourers, coming by at daybreak, observed the farmer still sleeping near a heap of stones by the roadside. Intending to assist him, they drew near, when the horse, by his grinning teeth and ready heels, showed them that it would be wiser to keep at a distance. He did not, probably, understand their humane intentions; but not till they had aroused the farmer, who at length got on his feet, would his equine guardian allow them to proceed.

Mrs. F—— mentions another instance of a high-spirited Irish horse, which, under similar circumstances, used to defend his master.

This man, a dissipated character, often coming home at night tipsy, would fall to the ground in a helpless state. Had the horse, while the man was in this condition, forsaken him, he would have been run over by any vehicle passing along the road; but the faithful horse was his vigilant guardian and protector. If nobody approached, the animal would stand patiently beside his prostrate master till he came to himself. He has been known to stand at his post during the whole of the night. If any one came near, he would gallop round him, kicking out his heels; or rearing and biting, if an attempt were made to touch him. Thus the man and animal changed places, the intelligent brute protecting both himself and his brutalized master.

I have a word to say even on this subject. Beware lest you take the first step which may lead you to become like the man I have described. You cannot expect, like him, to have a sagacious horse to watch over you. Yet, at the same time, do not be less faithful to an erring companion than were those noble steeds to their owners; watch over and protect him to the utmost. Learn to be kind to the thankful and to the unthankful.

JACK AND HIS DRIVER.

Mr. SMILES, in his Life of Rennie, tells us of a horse called Jack, who showed himself to be fully as sensible as the two animals just mentioned.

Jack's business was to draw the stone trucks along the tramway during the erection of Waterloo Bridge. Near at hand was a beershop, frequented by the navvies and carters. Jack's driver, named Tom, was an honest fellow, and very kind to Jack, but too fond of spending more time than he ought to have done in the beershop. Jack, though a restive animal, got accustomed to Tom's habits, and waited patiently till an overlooker startled him into activity. On one occasion, however, the superintendent being absent, Tom took so long a spell at the ale that Jack became restive, and the trace fastenings being long enough, the animal put his head inside the beerhouse door, and seizing the astonished Tom by the collar with his teeth, dragged him out to his duty at the truck. Great in consequence became the fame of Jack amongst the host of labourers.

Like famous Jack, do not hesitate to remind a friend of his duty, even though you have to seize him by the collar and drag him away to perform it.

THE HORSE WHICH FOUGHT FOR A DOG.

I HAVE given several instances of friendship existing between horses and dogs.

A fine hunter had formed a friendship with a handsome greyhound which slept in the stable with him, and generally accompanied him when taken out for exercise. When the greyhound accompanied his master in his walks, the horse would look over his shoulder, and neigh in a manner which plainly said, Let me go also; and when the dog returned, he was received with an unmistakable neigh of welcome. He would lick the horse's nose, and in return the horse would scratch his back with his teeth.

On one occasion the groom had, as usual, taken out the horse for exercise, followed by the greyhound, when a savage dog attacked the latter and bore him to the ground. The horse, seeing this, threw back his ears, and, breaking from the groom, rushed at the strange dog which was attacking his friend, seized him by the back with his teeth, speedily making him quit his hold, and shook him till a piece of his skin gave way. The offender, getting on his feet, scampered off, glad to escape from a foe who could punish him so severely.

THE ARAB STEED AND THE CHIEF.

M. DE LAMARTINE'S beautiful story of the Arab chief and his favourite steed has often been told. It shall form one of our anecdotes of horses.

A chief, Abou el Marek, and his marauding tribe, had one night attacked a caravan. When returning with their plunder, they were surrounded by the troops of the Pacha of Acre, who killed several, and bound the rest with cords. Abou el Marek, wounded and faint from loss of blood, was among the latter. Thus bound, while lying on the ground at night, he heard the neigh of his favourite steed, picketed at a short distance off. Anxious to caress the horse for the last time, he dragged himself up to him. "Poor friend," he said, "what will you do among these savage Turks? Shut up under the stifling roof of a khan, you will sicken and die. No longer will the women and children of the tent bring you barley, camel's milk, or *dhourra* in the hollow of their hands. No longer will you gallop free as the wind across the desert; no longer cleave the waters with your breast, and lave your sides in the pure stream. If I am to be a slave, at least you shall go free. Hasten back to our tent. Tell my wife that Abou el Marek will return no more!"

With these words, his hands being tied, the old chief undid, by means of his teeth, the rope which held the courser fast; but the noble animal, instead of galloping away to the desert, bent his head over his master, and seeing him helpless on the ground, took his clothes gently between his teeth, and, lifting him up, set off at full speed towards his distant home. Arriving there, he laid his master at the feet of his wife and children, and dropped down dead with fatigue.

What a brave example of affection, duty, and self-sacrifice! You may never be called on to perform the one hundredth part of the task undertaken willingly by that gallant Arab steed, but how are you carrying the tiny, light burdens which your every-day duties place on you? True heroism consists not so much in the performance of one noble deed, which may become the poet's theme, but in doing all that we have to do, and in seeking to do as much as we can of what there is to be done, to the very best of our power, and in bearing with patience what we are called on to bear.

THE OLD CHARGER.

THE horse has been frequently known to recognize his rider after a long absence. He is also especially a sociable animal, and once accustomed to others of his kind, rarely forgets them. At the trumpet's sound, the old war-horse pricks up his ears, snorts, and paws the ground, eager to join his ancient comrades.

Some years ago the assistant to a surveyor was employed to ride along a certain line of turnpike road, to see that the contractors were doing their work properly. He was mounted on a horse which had belonged to a field-officer; and, though aged, still possessed much spirit. It happened that a troop of yeomanry were out exercising on a neigh-

THE OLD CHARGER.

bouring common. No sooner did the old horse espy the
line of warriors, and hear the bugle-call, than, greatly to
the dismay of his rider, he leaped the fence and was speedily
at his post in front of the regiment; nor could the civilian
equestrian induce him by any means to quit the ground till
the regiment left it. As long as they kept the field, the
horse remained in front of the troop; and then insisted on
marching at their head into the town, prancing as well as
his old legs would allow him, to the great amusement of
the volunteers, and the no small annoyance of the clerk,
who had thus been compelled to assume a post he would
gladly have avoided.

Old habits cling to us as pertinaciously as did those of
that ancient war-steed; and often when we flatter ourselves
that they have been overcome, temptation appears, and we
yield to them as of yore. Do you, my young friends, take
heed to adopt only good habits, and adhere to them.

CHAPTER IV.

Donkeys.

EGRADED as it is supposed they are by nature, and cruelly ill-used as donkeys too often are in England, they are fully as intelligent as horses. They are not only capable of playing all manner of tricks, but sometimes indulge in a variety, of their own accord.

DONKEY BOB, THE POLICEMAN.

MRS. F——'s father-in-law had a donkey named Bob, which was kept in a field with other animals, and grazed quietly with them, but jealously guarded the entrance against all intruders. If any strange cows, sheep, or pigs ventured within his territory, Bob instantly ran at them full tilt, and hunted them from the premises, kicking out his heels and biting whenever he had the opportunity. Indeed, if he but saw them inclined to come in, he would stand in the gap and defend it bravely. His vigilance was so great that it was considered unnecessary to have a herdsman in the place.

Bob was clearly convinced that it was his duty to keep that field against all intruders. Dear young reader, when you have the property of another person to watch over, guard it as effectually as did honest Bob his master's paddock.

———❦———

THE ASS AND THE DOOR-LATCH.

DONKEYS sometimes exert their ingenuity to their own advantage, like some other creatures.

A certain ass had his quarters in a shed, in front of which was a small yard. On one side of the yard was a kitchen garden, separated from it by a wall, in which was a door fastened by two bolts and a latch. The owner of the premises one morning, in taking a turn round his garden, observed the footprints of an ass on the walks and beds. "Surely some one must have left the door open at night," thought the master. He accordingly took care to see that it was closed. Again, however, he found that the ass had visited the garden.

The next night, curious to know how this had happened, he watched from a window overlooking the yard. At first he kept a light burning near him. The ass, however, remained quietly at his stall. After a time, to enable him to see the better, he had it removed, when what was his surprise to see the supposed stupid donkey come out of the shed, go to the door, and, rearing himself on his hind-legs, unfasten the upper bolt of the door with his nose. This done, he next withdrew the lower bolt; then lifted the latch, and walked into the garden. He was not long

THE ASS AND THE DOOR-LATCH.

engaged in his foraging expedition, and soon returned with a bunch of carrots in his mouth. Placing them in his shed, he went back and carefully closed the door, and began at his ease to munch the provender he had so adroitly got possession of.

The owner, suspecting that people would not believe his story, invited several of his neighbours to witness the performance of the ass. Not till the light, however, had been taken away, would the creature commence his operations, evidently conscious that he was doing wrong. A lock was afterwards put on the door, which completely baffled the ingenuity of the cunning animal.

THE ASS AND THE TEETOTALLER.

THE ass has a memory not inferior to that of the horse. This was especially noticeable in the case of an ass belonging to a carrier at Wigan.

The ass and his master were accustomed to stop at a certain public-house, where the latter obtained a pot of beer, of which he always allowed the animal a little. At length the master turned teetotaller, when his principles forbade him to stop at the public-house; but the ass, whenever he reached the usual halting-place, refused to go on, and no beating would induce him to do so till he had received his usual allowance of beer. The carrier was therefore obliged to buy some beer for his beast, though no longer requiring it himself.

Remember what I said before about bad habits. Though

your friends from weariness may cease to rebuke you, it is
no proof that you are cured of them, or that the habits are
not as objectionable as at the first.

THE DONKEY AND HIS MISTRESS.

DONKEYS are capable of great affection for those who treat
them well.

An old woman, known to Mrs. F——, had a donkey
which usually grazed on the roadside near her cottage, and
when he saw any person about to enter her abode would
instantly run to the door and defend it against all intrusion
till the dame herself appeared. If any one annoyed the
old woman—as the boys around would sometimes do, for
the sake of seeing how the donkey would behave—he
would kick out at them fiercely, put them to the rout,
and pursue them for some distance.

When the dame wished to ride, he would proceed with
the greatest care and gentleness; but if any other person
attempted to mount him, the ass very soon convinced them
that their will and power were useless in a contest, and the
effort usually ended in the rider being roughly thrown, and
perhaps kicked.

THE BRAVE ASS AND HIS FOE.

I HAVE heard of a donkey which on one occasion bravely
did battle for himself.

He happened to be feeding near a river when a fierce bull-dog attacked him ; but so gallantly did he strike out with his heels, that his assailant was unable to fix on him. At length the ass suddenly turned round and seized the neck of the bull-dog in his teeth. The dog howled with pain, and struggled to get free, but the ass had no intention as yet of letting it go. Holding it tight, he dragged it struggling into the water, going in deeper and deeper ; then kneeling down where the depth was sufficient for the purpose, he kept the dog under the surface till it was drowned.

Whenever you are attacked by a spiritual or moral foe, imitate the brave ass, and drown it.

THE BAKER'S DONKEY.

I MET some time ago with an account of a clever donkey which was employed in drawing a baker's cart. He was so well acquainted with the houses of all his master's customers, that while the baker went into one to deliver his loaves, the sagacious ass would proceed to the door of the next, at which, when he could reach the knocker, he gave a rap-a-tap-tap. If unable to do so, he would stamp with his feet in a peculiar way, well known to the inmates. He never failed to stop at their doors, nor was he ever known by mistake to go to the wrong house.

Be as careful to learn your school lessons now, and as exact in business matters when you grow up, as was the baker's donkey to attend to what he conceived his duty.

THE BRAVE ASS AND HIS FOE

THE SHIPWRECKED ASS.

AN ass was shipped at Gibraltar on board the *Isis* frigate, to be sent to Captain Dundas, then at Malta. The ship, on her voyage, struck on a sand-bank off Cape de Gat, when among other things thrown overboard was the poor ass; it being hoped that, although the sea was running high, the animal might reach the shore.

A few days afterwards, when the gates of Gibraltar were opened in the morning, the guard was surprised to see the ass present himself for admittance. On being allowed to pass, he went immediately to the stable of his former master. Not only had the animal swam safely to shore through the heavy surf, but, without guide or compass, had found his way from Cape de Gat to Gibraltar, a distance of more than two hundred miles, across a mountainous and intricate country, intersected by streams, and in so short a time that he could not have made one false turn.

THE OLD HAWKER AND HIS DONKEY.

AN old hawker was in the habit of traversing the country with his ass, which had served him faithfully for many years. To help himself along, he used frequently to catch hold of the animal's tail.

The winter wind was blowing strongly, and snow had long been falling heavily, when the old hawker found himself suddenly plunged with the ass into a deep drift. In

THE SHIPWRECKED ASS.

vain he struggled to get out, and fully believed that his last hour had come. The ass succeeded better, and reached the road; but after looking about and finding his master missing, he once more made his way through the drift, and then, placing himself in a position which enabled the old hawker to catch hold of his tail, the faithful beast dragged him safely out.

Never despise the help offered by a humble friend. We are all apt to over-estimate our own strength and wisdom.

THE MUSICAL ASS.

WE have no less an authority than Dr. Franklin to prove that donkeys enjoy music.

The mistress of a chateau in France where he visited had an excellent voice, and every time she began to sing, a donkey belonging to the establishment invariably came near the window, and listened with the greatest attention. One day, during the performance of a piece of music which apparently pleased it more than any it had previously heard, the animal, quitting its usual post outside the window, unceremoniously entered the room, and, to exhibit its satisfaction, began to bray with all its might.

I need scarcely hint, after you have read this story, that you will act wisely in keeping your proper place. You may be esteemed wonderfully clever in the nursery, or even at school; but when you appear among strangers at home, or go out visiting, wait till you are invited to exhibit your talents, or you may be considered as audacious a donkey as was the musical ass.

I think I have told you anecdotes enough to show that donkeys are not such stupid creatures as is generally supposed; and I am very sure that, if they were better treated, their character would rise much in public estimation.

CHAPTER V.

Elephants.

WE have, I think, sufficient evidence to prove that elephants are more sagacious, and possessed of greater reasoning power, than any other animals. They seem, indeed, to have many of the feelings of human beings. In spite of their size, what activity do they exhibit! what wonderful judgment! How cautious they are in all their proceedings! How great is their love of regularity and good order! So gentle, too, are many of them, that the youngest infant might be safely entrusted to their keeping; and yet, if insulted or annoyed by a grown-up person, the same animal might hurl him to the ground with a blow of his trunk, or crush him with his ponderous feet. I will tell you a few of the numerous stories I have heard about these wonderful creatures.

THE ELEPHANT IN A WELL.

WHILE the British troops were besieging Bhurtpore in India, the water in the ponds and tanks in the neighbourhood be-

THE ELEPHANT IN A WELL.

coming exhausted, it could only be obtained from deep and large wells. In this service elephants were especially useful.

One day two of these animals,—one of them large and strong, the other much smaller,—came together to a well. The smaller elephant carried by his trunk a bucket, which the larger, not having one, stole from him. The smaller animal knew that he could not wrest it from the other, but he eyed him, watching for an opportunity of avenging himself. The larger elephant now approached the edge of the well, when the smaller one, rushing forward with all his might, pushed him fairly into the water.

Ludicrous as was the scene, the consequences might have been disastrous. Should the huge animal not be got out, the water would be spoiled; at all events, his floundering about would make it very muddy. The elephant, however, seemed in no way disconcerted, and kept floating at his ease, enjoying the cool liquid, and exhibiting no wish to come out of it. At length a number of fascines used in the siege were brought, and these being lowered into the well, the elephant was induced by his driver to place them under his feet. In this way a pile was raised sufficiently high to enable him to stand upon it. But, being unwilling to leave the water, he after a time would allow no more fascines to be lowered; and his driver had to caress him, and promise him plenty of arrack as a reward, to induce him to raise himself out of the water. Thus incited, the elephant permitted more fascines to be thrown in; and at length, after some masonry was removed from the margin of the well, he was able to step out—the whole operation having occupied fourteen hours.

You will probably smile at the conduct of the two huge creatures. It was curiously like that of human beings. A big boy plays a smaller one a trick—snatches something from him. The other retaliates. An uproar is raised, and often serious inconvenience follows. These two elephants behaved just like two ill-tempered boys; and through them a whole army was doomed to suffer for many hours the pangs of thirst. Remember the golden rule, "Do unto others as you would that they should do unto you."

THE ELEPHANT ACCUSING HIS DRIVER OF THEFT.

THE following anecdote shows the elephant's perception of what is right.

A large elephant was sent a few years ago to assist in piling up timber at Nagercoil. The officer who despatched it, suspecting the honesty of the driver, requested the wife of a missionary, to whose house the animal was sent, to watch that he received his proper allowance of rice. After some time the lady, suspecting that her charge was being defrauded of his rice, intimated her mistrust to the keeper, who, pretending surprise at having such an imputation made against him, exclaimed in his native tongue, "Madam, do you think I would rob my child?" The elephant, which was standing by, seemed aware of the subject of the conversation, and kept eying the keeper, who had on a bulky waist-cloth; and no sooner had he uttered these words than the animal threw his trunk round him, and untying the waist-cloth, a quantity of rice fell to the ground.

THE ELEPHANT AND THE TIPSY SOLDIER.

SOME years ago a soldier, stationed at Pondicherry, formed a friendship with an elephant, to whom he used to give a portion of his daily allowance of liquor. One day the soldier, getting tipsy, and being followed by the guard, ran to hide himself behind the elephant, under whose body he was in a few minutes fast asleep. The guard approached to seize the delinquent, but, though the keeper assisted the soldiers, the elephant would allow no one to come near him, and kept whirling his trunk about in a way which showed that he was determined to protect his charge at all costs.

What was the soldier's horror next morning, when, looking up, he found the huge animal standing over him! One step of his monstrous feet, and his life would have been crushed out. If he did not then and there resolve to abjure intoxicating liquor for the future, he deserved to be less fortunate another time. As he crawled out, the elephant evidently perceived the terror he was in, and, to reassure him, caressed him gently with his trunk, and signified that he might go to his quarters. The animal now seeing his friend in safety, suffered his keeper to approach and lead him away.

Gratitude prompted the elephant to protect his erring friend. How sad to think that human beings are so often less grateful to those from whom they have received benefits!

THE ELEPHANT AND THE TIPSY SOLDIER.

ELEPHANTS HELPING EACH OTHER.

WHEN an army marches in India, elephants are employed in carrying field-pieces, levelling roads, piling up timber, fetching water; all of which, and many other occupations, they perform with a regularity which shows that they understand what they are about. Formerly, indeed, they were often trained to launch ships, by pushing them off the stocks with the weight of their huge bodies.

Some troops, on their march, had to cross a steep and rugged hill. This could only be done by cutting away portions, and laying trees to fill up the chasms. The first elephant, when conducted up to this roughly-formed road, shook his head, and roared piteously, evidently convinced that it was insecure. On some alteration being made he recommenced his examination, by pressing with his trunk the trees that had been thrown across. After this he advanced a fore-leg with great caution, raising the fore-part of his body so as to throw the weight on the trunk. Thus he examined every tree and rock as he proceeded, while frequently no force could induce him to advance till some alteration he desired had been made. On his reaching the top his delight was evident. He caressed his keepers, and threw the dirt about in a playful manner.

A younger elephant had to follow. The first watched his ascent with the most intense interest, making motions all the while as though he was assisting him, by shouldering him up the declivity. As the latter neared the top, a difficult spot had to be passed, when the first, approaching, extended his trunk to the assistance of his brother in distress. The younger, entwining his round it, was thus led up to the summit in safety. The first on this evinced his delight by giving a salute something like the sound of a trumpet. The two animals then greeted each other as if they had been long separated, and had just met after accomplishing a perilous achievement. They mutually embraced, and stood face to face for a considerable time, as if whispering congratulations. The driver then made them salaam to the general, who ordered them five rupees each for sweetmeats. On this they immediately returned thanks by another salaam.

Can you, after reading this, ever refuse to help any human beings in distress? Imitate, too, that sagacious elephant, in never venturing on unsafe ground. Look before you leap.

THE ELEPHANT AND THE ROTTEN BRIDGE.

IT is seldom that an elephant can be induced to pass over ground he considers unsafe. Sometimes, however, a driver obtains such a mastery over a timid animal, that he compels him to undertake what his better sense would induce him to decline.

An elephant of this character was owned by a person residing in the neighbourhood of Gyah. Between the house and the town was a small bridge, over which the elephant had frequently passed. One day, however, he refused to go over. He tried it with his trunk, evidently suspecting that its strength was not sufficient to bear his weight. Still, the obstinate driver urged him on with the sharp spear with which elephants are driven. At length, with cautious steps he began the passage, still showing an extreme unwillingness to proceed. As he approached the centre, loud cracks were heard, when the treacherous bridge gave way, and both elephant and rider were precipitated into the stream below; the latter being killed by the fall, and the former, who had proved himself the most sensible being of the two, being much injured.

Let no force induce you to do what is wrong. All bad ways are like that rotten bridge. When others attempt to goad you on to do evil, tell them the story of the elephant and the rotten bridge.

THE ELEPHANT TURNED NURSE.

WHO would expect to see a huge elephant take care of a delicate little child? Yet more vigilant and gentle nurses cannot be found than are some of these animals.

The wife of a mahout, or elephant driver, was frequently in the habit of giving her baby in charge of an elephant. The child would begin, as soon as it was left to itself, to crawl about, getting sometimes under the elephant's huge legs, at others becoming entangled among the branches on which he was feeding. On such occasions the elephant would gently disengage the child, by lifting it with his trunk or removing the boughs. The elephant, it should be said, was himself chained by the leg to the stump of a tree. When the child had crawled nearly to the limits of his range, he would advance his trunk, and lift it back as ten-

THE ELEPHANT AND THE ROTTEN BRIDGE.

derly as possible to the spot whence it had started. Indeed, no nurse could have attended an infant with more good sense and care than did this elephant his master's child.

THE WOUNDED ELEPHANT AND THE SURGEON.

To conclude my anecdotes about elephants, I must tell you two which show, even more than the other incidents I have mentioned, the wonderful sense they possess.

An elephant had been severely wounded, and submitting to have his wound dressed, used, after two or three times, to go alone to the hospital and extend himself, so that the surgeon could easily reach the injured part. Though the pain the animal suffered was so severe that he often uttered the most plaintive groans, he never interrupted the operation, but exhibited every token of submission to the surgeon, till his cure was effected.

Still more curious is the following :—A young elephant which had accompanied its mother to the battle-field received a severe wound in the head. Nothing could induce it to allow the injury to be attended to. At length, by certain signs and words, the keeper explained to the mother what was wanted. The sagacious animal immediately seized the young one with her trunk, and, though it groaned with agony, held it to the ground, while the surgeon was thus enabled to dress the wound. Day after day she continued to act in the same way, till the wound was perfectly healed.

CHAPTER VI.

Oxen.

THE virtues of cows are more active than passive. I may sum them up by saying that they are very affectionate mothers, and will sometimes, like horses and dogs, find their way across the country to the spot where they have been bred.

THE PROUD COW.

MRS. F—— told me the following anecdote:—Her father had four cows, which every evening, at milking-time, were driven from the field into their byre. On their way they had to pass through the farm-yard, when they would endeavour to snatch as many mouthfuls of hay as they had time to secure from the hay-stacks. One especially, who was accustomed to take the lead of the other cows, was more particularly addicted to this trick. She was thus sometimes the last to be driven into the byre. When, however, she found that her three companions had entered before her, nothing would induce her to follow them. She would stand with her fore-legs just over the threshold, stretch forth her neck, and moo angrily; but further than this, neither coaxing, blows, nor the barking of the dog at her heels, would induce her to go. The contest always ended in the rest of the cows being driven out; when she would at once take the lead, and walk quietly into her stall without the least persuasion. The dairy-maid called her the Proud Cow.

Another Irish cow has been known to act in a similar manner.

So her pride brought Mistress Cow many a whack on the back. Depend on it, if you stand on your dignity, you may often suffer, as she did.

THE COW AND HER TORMENTOR.

IN my younger days, I had a companion who used to catch our tutor's cow by the tail, and make her drag him at full speed round and round the field. One day, when he was quietly walking along the path to church, the cow espied him, and making chase, very nearly caught him with her horns as he leaped over the nearest gate.

I will tell you of another cow, which was frequently annoyed by a boy amusing himself with throwing stones at her. She had borne his mischief for some time, when at length, making after him, she hooked the end of her horns into his clothes, lifted him from the ground, carried him out of the field, and laid him down in the road. She then,

THE COW AND HER TORMENTOR.

satisfied with the gentle punishment she had inflicted, returned calmly to her pasture.

A COW SEEKING HER CALF.

Cows have as much affection for their young as have other
animals, and it is piteous to hear them mooing when deprived of their calves.

A cow had her calf taken from her, and left at Bushy
Park, while she was driven off to Smithfield to be sold.
The following morning, when it was supposed the cow was
in London, she appeared at the gate of the yard in which
her calf was confined. Influenced by her love for her offspring, she had broken out of the pen, passed through all
the streets of the suburbs without being stopped by the
police, who naturally supposed, from her quiet demeanour,
that the drover must be at her heels; and once in the
country, had quickly traversed the twelve miles which took
her to her former home. It is probable that she traversed
the same road to Bushy which she had followed when being
driven from that place to Smithfield.

In Africa, the Hottentot shepherds employ a species of
cow to guard their flocks of sheep. They keep the animals
together with all the sagacity of Scotch sheep-dogs, and will
attack with the utmost bravery any enemy attempting to
injure them.

What difficulties does true love overcome! If that poor
dull cow could feel such love for her offspring as to overcome the usual apathy of her kind, what must be the feel-

ings of a human mother towards her children! Can you, then, ever carelessly wound yours by your misconduct?

A SAVAGE BULL TAMED BY KINDNESS.

A SAVAGE bull was kept in a farm-yard constantly chained on account of its fierceness. A gentleman who went to stay at the farm was an especial object of dislike to the animal.

One night, during a tremendous storm of thunder and lightning, the bull was heard to roar piteously, evidently alarmed at the strife of the elements. The servants were ordered to lead the bull from its open shed into a close stable, where it would be less exposed; but they were afraid to go. The visitor, therefore, compassionating the animal, although it had shown itself his determined foe, went out into the yard. Here he found the bull lying on its back; having, in its struggles to get free, almost torn the ring through the gristle of its nose. No sooner did he appear than the creature rose, and by its fawning actions showed how delighted it was to obtain the companionship of a human being. Now quiet as a lamb, it allowed the stranger to lead it into the stable; and the next morning, when he went to visit it, it endeavoured to express its gratitude by rubbing its nose against him.

From that day forward it always treated him as a friend, while it remained as savage as before towards every one else.

There are times when the most savage hearts can be

touched. Wait for them, and then apply the soothing balm of gentleness.

THE FAITHFUL BUFFALO.

FEROCIOUS in aspect as is the long hairy-skinned buffalo—or properly the bison—of America, and savage when attacked, yet it is capable of devoted affection towards its own kind.

A party of hunters were riding on the prairies, when two fine buffalo-bulls were seen proceeding along the opposite side of a stream. One of the hunters took aim at the nearest buffalo, which was crossing with his haunches towards him. The ball broke the animal's right hip, and he plunged away on three legs, the other hanging useless. The hunter, leaping on his horse, put spurs to its flanks, and in three minutes he and his companions were close on the bull. To his astonishment, and the still greater surprise of two older hunters, the unhurt bull stuck to his comrade's side without flinching. He fired another shot, which took effect in the lungs of the first buffalo. The second sheered off for a moment, but instantly returned to his friend. The wounded buffalo became distressed, and slackened his pace. The unwounded one not only retarded his, but coming to the rear of his friend, stood with his head down, offering battle.

Here indeed was devotion! The sight was, to all three of the hunters, a sublime one. They could no more have accepted the challenge of this brave creature, than they could have smitten Damon at the side of Pythias. The wounded buffalo ran on to the border of the next marsh,

A SAVAGE BULL TAMED BY KINDNESS.

and, in attempting to cross, fell headlong down the steep bank. Not till that moment, when courage was useless, did his faithful companion seek his own safety in flight. The hunters took off their hats, and gave three parting cheers, as he vanished on the other side of the wood.

THE AFFECTIONATE BUFFALO-BULL.

THE cow-buffaloes are frequently attracted by a ruse of the Indians, which they call "making a calf." One of the party covers himself with a buffalo-skin, and another with the skin of a wolf. They then creep on all-fours within sight of the buffaloes, when the pretended wolf jumps on the back of the pretended calf, which bellows in imitation of the real one, crying for assistance.

A white man and an Indian were hunting together. At length a solitary bull and cow were seen in the distance. After the Indian personating the calf had bellowed a short time, the cow ran forward, and attempted to spring towards the hunters; but the bull, seeming to understand the trick, tried to stop her by running between them. The cow now dodged and got round him, and ran within ten or fifteen yards of them, with the bull close at her heels, when both men fired, and brought her down. The bull instantly stopped short, and bending over her, tried to help her up with his nose, evincing the most persevering affection for her; nor could they get rid of him, so as to cut up the cow, without shooting him also—a cruel reward to the noble animal for his conjugal affection.

THE KIND OX AND THE SHEEP.

This account, which is mentioned by Mr. Kane the artist, and that previously given, show that these animals are capable of great affection for each other, though in general they leave their wounded comrades to shift for themselves.

THE KIND OX AND THE SHEEP.

I HAVE to tell you of an instance of the benevolence of an ox. Oxen may possess many virtues, but are not in the habit of making a parade of them. Sheep are sometimes seized with fits, when they fall on their back, and are unable of themselves to regain their legs. While in this helpless position, they are sometimes attacked by birds of prey, which tear out their eyes, and otherwise injure them.

An unfortunate sheep had fallen in the way I have described, and was in vain endeavouring to struggle to its feet, when an ox, grazing near, observed what had happened. Going up to it, it carefully turned the animal over on its side; and when it had regained its feet, walked away, and went on feeding as before, satisfied that it had done what was wanted.

My young friends, try to help those in distress, though there may be as much difference between you and them as between that ox and the sheep.

THE COURAGEOUS BULL.

I REMEMBER meeting with an account of a bull, which fed on the savannahs of Central America. He had gored so many cattle, that he was at length caught with a lasso, and to prevent him doing further mischief, the tips of his horns were blunted. Some weeks after, a cow belonging to his herd was found killed by a jaguar, and from the state of the bull's head and neck, which were fearfully torn, it was evident that he had fought bravely for the animals under his care. It was now seen that it would have been wiser not to have deprived the defender of the herd of his weapons.

To enable him to do battle in future, he was secured, his wounds were dressed, and his horns made sharp again. The body of the cow having been preserved from the birds and beasts of prey during the day, the gallant bull was turned out again in the evening. The jaguar, as was expected, returned at night, when a furious battle took place. The next morning the jaguar was found dead, pierced through and through, close by the cow; while the bull, which stood near, bleeding from many a wound, was seen to rush, ever and anon, against his now helpless antagonist.

THE BRAVE BULL AND THE WISE PIG.

A PIG had been stolen by two men, who were driving it at night along an unfrequented path in the neighbourhood of Rotherham. As the pig squeaked loudly, they feared they might be betrayed, and were about to kill it. The pig, however, struggled violently, and had already received a wound, when it managed to escape into a neighbouring field, squeaking still louder, and with the blood flowing from its wound. The robbers, pursuing the pig, found themselves face to face with a large bull, which had been till now grazing quietly. Apparently understanding the state of affairs, and compassionating, it may be presumed, the pig, he ran fiercely at the men, compelling them to fly for their lives. It was only, indeed, by leaping desperately over a hedge, that they escaped an ugly toss from the horns of the animal.

In vain did they wait, in the hope of recovering the pig. Piggy, having found a powerful friend, was too wise to desert him, and kept close to his heels, till the crowing of the cocks in the neighbouring farms warned the robbers to make their escape.

THE BRAVE BULL AND THE WISE PIG.

CHAPTER VII.

Savage and Other Animals.

THE LION AND HIS KEEPER.

THE majestic step, the bold look, the grace and strength of the lion, have obtained for him the title of "king of beasts." He is greatly indebted, however, to the imagination of the poet for the noble qualities which he is supposed to possess. He is, though capable of gratitude towards those from whom he has received kindness, often treacherous and revengeful, and Dr. Livingstone considers him an arrant coward. The stories, however, which I have to narrate, describe his better qualities.

Mrs. Lee tells us of a lion which was kept in the menagerie at Brussels. The animal's cell requiring some repairs, the keeper led him to the upper portion of it, where, after playing with him for some time, they both fell asleep. The carpenter, who was employed in the work below, wishing to ascertain whether it was finished as desired, called the keeper to inspect what he had done. Receiving no answer, he climbed up, when, seeing the

THE GENEROUS LION AND HIS ASSAILANTS.

keeper and lion thus asleep side by side, he uttered a cry of horror.   His voice awoke the lion, which, gazing fiercely at him for a moment, placed his paw on the breast of his keeper, and lay down to sleep again.

On the other attendants being summoned, they aroused the keeper, who, on opening his eyes, appeared in no way frightened, but taking the paw of the lion, shook it, and quietly led him down to the lower part of the den.

THE GENEROUS LION AND HIS ASSAILANTS.

THE custom existed till lately on the Continent of having combats between wild animals and dogs, although they were very different from the spectacles exhibited in the days of ancient Rome.

It had been arranged that a battle should take place between a lion and four large bull-dogs.   The lion, released from his den, stood looking round him in the arena, when the dogs were let loose.   Three of them, however, turned tail, one alone having the courage to attack him.   The lion, crouching down as the dog approached, stretched him motionless with one stroke of his paw ; then drawing the animal towards him, almost concealed him with his huge fore-paws.   It was believed that the dog was dead.   In a short time, however, it began to move, and was allowed by the lion to struggle up on to its feet ; but when the dog attempted to run away, the lion, with two bounds, reached it, showing it how completely it was in his power.

Pity, or it may have been contempt, now seemed to

move the heart of the generous lion. He stepped back a few paces, and allowed the dog to escape through the door opened for the purpose, while the spectators uttered loud shouts of applause.

THE GRATEFUL LION.

A REMARKABLY handsome African lion was being sent to the coast, where it was to be placed on board ship, to be carried to France, when it fell ill. Its keepers, supposing that it would not recover, left it to die on the wild open side of the mountain which they were at the time crossing. There it lay, on the point of perishing, when a traveller, who had been shooting in the interior of the country, happened to pass that way. Seeing the condition of the noble-looking animal, he gave it some new milk from the goats which he had in his camp. The lion drank it eagerly, and at once began to revive, showing his gratitude by licking the hand of the benevolent stranger. The traveller continued his kind offices to the poor beast, which, in consequence of his care, completely recovered.

When the traveller moved on, the lion accompanied his camp, and became so attached to his benefactor that he followed him about everywhere, taking food from his hand, and being in every respect as tame as a dog.

THE TIGER AND HIS COMPANIONS.

ON one of her voyages from China, the *Pitt*, East India-man, had on board, among her passengers, a young tiger. He appeared to be as harmless and playful as a kitten, and allowed the utmost familiarity from every one. He was especially fond of creeping into the sailors' hammocks; and while he lay stretched on the deck, he would suffer two or three of them to place their heads on his back, as upon a pillow. Now and then, however, he would at dinner-time run off with pieces of their meat; and though some-times severely punished for the theft, he bore the chastisement he received with the patience of a dog. His chief companion was a terrier, with whom he would play all sorts of tricks—tumbling and rolling over the animal in the most amusing manner, without hurting it. He would also frequently run out on the bowsprit, and climb about the rigging with the agility of a cat.

On his arrival in England, he was sent to the menagerie at the Tower. While there, another terrier was introduced into his den. Possibly he may have mistaken it for his old friend, for he immediately became attached to the dog, and appeared uneasy whenever it was taken away. Now and then the dangerous experiment was tried of allowing the terrier to remain while the tiger was fed. Presuming on their friendship, the dog occasionally ventured to approach him; but the tiger showed his true nature on such occasions, by snarling in a way which made the little animal quickly retreat.

THE TIGER AND HIS COMPANIONS.

He had been in England two years, when one of the seamen of the *Pitt* came to the Tower. The animal at once recognized his old friend, and appeared so delighted, that the sailor begged to be allowed to go into the den. The tiger, on this, rubbed himself against him, licked his hands, and fawned on him as a cat would have done. The sailor remained in the den for a couple of hours or more, during which time the tiger kept so close to him, that it was evident he would have some difficulty in getting out again, without the animal making his escape at the same time. The den consisted of two compartments. At last the keeper contrived to entice the tiger to the inner one, when he closed the slide, and the seaman was liberated.

Great is the danger of associating with those of bad morals—pleasant and friendly as they may seem.

THE TIGRESS AND HER YOUNG.

THE tigress generally takes much less care of her young than does the lioness of her whelps. Occasionally, however, she shows the same maternal affection.

Two young tiger cubs had been found by some villagers, while their mother had been ranging in quest of prey. They were put into a stable, where, during the whole night, they continued to make the greatest possible noise. After some days, during which it was evident that their mother had been searching for them in every direction, she at length discovered the place where they were confined, and replied to their cries with tremendous howlings. The keeper, fearing she would break into the stable, and probably wreak her vengeance on his head, set the cubs at liberty. She at once made her way to them, and before morning had carried them off to an adjoining jungle.

If that savage tigress could thus risk the loss of her life for the sake of her cubs, think what must be your mother's love for you. Do you try to repay her in some part for all her care and tenderness, by your affection, by doing all she wishes, and what you know is right, whether she sees you or not; trying not in any way to vex her, but to please her in all things?

THE WOLF AND HIS MASTER.

EVEN a wolf, savage as that animal is, may, if caught young, and treated kindly, become tame.

A story is told of a wolf which showed a considerable amount of affection for its master. He had brought it up from a puppy, and it became as tame as the best-trained dog, obeying him in everything. Having frequently to leave home, and not being able to take the wolf with him, he sent it to a menagerie, where he knew it would be carefully looked after. At first the wolf was very unhappy, and evidently pined for its absent master. At length, resigning itself to its fate, it made friends with its keepers; and recovered its spirits.

Fully eighteen months had passed by, when its old master, returning home, paid a visit to the menagerie. Immediately he spoke, the wolf recognized his voice, and made strenuous efforts to get free. On being set at liberty, it sprang forward, and leaped up and caressed him like a dog. Its master, however, left it with its keepers, and three years passed away before he paid another visit to the menagerie. Notwithstanding this lapse of time, the wolf again recognized him, and exhibited the same marks of affection.

On its master again going away, the wolf became gloomy and desponding, and refused its food, so that fears were entertained for its life. It recovered its health, however, and though it suffered its keepers to approach, exhibited the savage disposition of its tribe towards all strangers.

The history of this wolf shows you that the fiercest tempers may be calmed by gentleness.

FOXES : THEIR DOMESTIC HABITS.

ARRANT thieves as foxes are, with regard to their domestic virtues Mrs. F—— assures me that they eminently shine. Both parents take the greatest interest in rearing and educating their offspring. They provide, in their burrow, a comfortable nest, lined with feathers, for their new-born cubs. Should either parent perceive in the neighbourhood of their abode the slightest sign of human approach, they immediately carry their young to a spot of greater safety, sometimes many miles away. They usually set off in the twilight of a fine evening. The papa fox having taken a survey all round, marches first, the young ones march singly, and mamma brings up the rear. On reaching a wall or bank, papa always mounts first, and looks carefully

THE WOLF AND HIS MASTER.

around, rearing himself on his haunches to command a wider view. He then utters a short cry, which the young ones, understanding as "Come along!" instantly obey. All being safely over, mamma follows, pausing in her turn on the top of the fence, when she makes a careful survey, especially rearward. She then gives a responsive cry, answering to "All right!" and follows the track of the others. Thus the party proceed on their march, repeating the same precautions at each fresh barrier.

When peril approaches, the wary old fox instructs his young ones to escape with turns and doublings on their path, while he himself will stand still on some brow or knoll, where he can both see and be seen. Having thus drawn attention to himself, he will take to flight in a different direction. Occasionally, while the young family are disporting themselves near their home, if peril approach, the parents utter a quick, peculiar cry, commanding the young ones to hurry to earth; knowing that, in case of pursuit, they have neither strength nor speed to secure their escape. They themselves will then take to flight, and seek some distant place of security.

The instruction they afford their young is varied. Sometimes the parents toss bones into the air for the young foxes to catch. If the little one fails to seize it before it falls to the ground, the parent will snap at him in reproof. If he catches it cleverly, papa growls his approval, and tosses it up again. This sport continues for a considerable time.

As I have said, no other animals so carefully educate their young in the way they should go, as does the fox. He is a good husband, an excellent father, capable of friendship, and a very intelligent member of society; but all the while, it must be confessed, an incorrigible rogue and thief.

Do not pride yourself on being perfect because you possess some good qualities. Consider the many bad ones which counteract them, and strive to overcome those.

THE FOX AND THE WILD-FOWL.

MRS. F—— gave me the following account of the ingenious stratagem of a fox, witnessed by a friend.

He was lying one summer's day under the shelter of some shrubs on the banks of the Tweed, when his attention was attracted by the cries of wild-fowl, accompanied by a great deal of fluttering and splashing. On looking round, he perceived a large brood of ducks, which had been disturbed by the drifting of a fir branch among them. After circling in the air for a little time, they again settled down on their feeding-ground.

Two or three minutes elapsed, when the same event again occurred. A branch drifted down with the stream into the midst of the ducks, and startled them from their repast. Once more they rose upon the wing, clamouring loudly, but when the harmless bough had drifted by, settled themselves down upon the water as before. This occurred so frequently, that at last they scarcely troubled themselves to flutter out of the way, even when about to be touched by the drifting bough.

The gentleman, meantime, marking the regular intervals

at which the fir branches succeeded each other in the same track, looked for a cause, and perceived, at length, higher up the bank of the stream, a fox, which, having evidently sent them adrift, was eagerly watching their progress and the effect they produced. Satisfied with the result, cunning Reynard at last selected a larger branch of spruce-fir than usual, and couching himself down on it, set it adrift as he had done the others. The birds, now well trained to indifference, scarcely moved till he was in the midst of them, when, making rapid snaps right and left, he secured two fine young ducks as his prey, and floated forward triumphantly on his raft; while the surviving fowls, clamouring in terror, took to flight, and returned no more to the spot.

THE LABOURER AND THE SLY FOX.

A LABOURER going to his work one morning, caught sight of a fox stretched out at full length under a bush. Believing it to be dead, the man drew it out by the tail, and swung it about to assure himself of the fact. Perceiving no symptoms of life, he then threw it over his shoulder, intending to make a cap of the skin, and ornament his cottage wall with the brush. While the fox hung over one shoulder, his mattock balanced it on the other. The point of the instrument, as he walked along, every now and then struck against the ribs of the fox, which, not so dead as the man supposed, objected to this proceeding, though he did not mind being carried along with his head downward. Losing patience, he gave a sharp snap at that portion of the

THE FOX AND THE WILD-FOWL.

labourer's body near which his head hung. The man, startled by this sudden attack, threw fox and mattock to the ground, when, turning round, he espied the live animal making off at full speed.

THE FOX IN THE HEN-ROOST.

I CANNOT help fancying that Irish foxes are even more cunning than their brethren in other parts of the world, I have heard so many accounts of their wonderful doings.

Near Buttevant, where some of Mrs. F——'s family resided, there happened to be a hole in the thatch of the fowl-house. A fox, finding it out, sprang down through the aperture, and slew and feasted all the night to his heart's desire. The intruder, however, had not reflected that he might be unable to secure his retreat by the way through which he had entered—*facilis descensus averni*.

To spring upward, especially after a heavy supper, was a laborious effort; and no doubt the villain had grown sufficiently uneasy in his mind before the early hour at which the farm-servant opened the door to liberate the fowls. When the door was opened, the man beheld the poacher in the midst of his slaughtered game. Cudgel in hand, he sprang in and fastened the door behind him, ready for a duel with Master Reynard at close quarters. But well the rascal knew that discretion is the better part of valour, and that

> " He who fights and runs away,
> May live to fight another day."

So, after being hunted about the house for some time, he

seized an opportunity, when the man stooped to aim a decisive blow at him, to spring upon his assailant's back, and thence leap through the aperture in the roof, which he could not otherwise have reached. Thus he made his escape.

It would have been amusing to see the countenance of the man, when he found his fancied victim vanish from his sight like the wizard of a fairy tale.

Cunning rogues often get trapped, like the fox, when they hope to enjoy their spoil in security. Beware, when you have such an one to deal with, that he does not spring on your back, and leave you to be answerable for his crime.

To you, my young friend, I would say—You cannot be too cautious in dealing with what is wrong. You may fancy yourself able to cope with it, but it may prove too cunning for you. Better keep out of its way, till you have gained strength and wisdom.

THE FOX IN A PLOUGH FURROW.

THE hero of Scotch story escaped from his foes by making his way down the course of a stream, that no trace of his footsteps might be found. Equally sagacious was an Irish fox, which, pursued by the hounds, was seen by a farmer, while he was ploughing a field, to run along in the furrow directly before him. While wondering how it was that the sly creature was pursuing this course, he heard the cry of dogs, and turning round, saw the whole pack at a dead stand, near the other end of the field, at the very spot where Reynard had entered the newly-formed trench. The fox had evidently taken this ingenious way of eluding pursuit; and the farmer, admiring the cleverness of the animal, allowed it to get off without betraying its whereabouts.

THE FOX AND THE BADGER.

LONG live Old Ireland! A countryman was making his way along the bank of a mountain stream in Galway, when he caught sight of a badger moving leisurely along a ledge of rock on the opposite bank. The sound of the huntsman's horn at the same moment reached his ears, followed by the well-known cry of a pack of dogs. As he was looking round, to watch for their approach, he caught sight of a fox making his way behind the badger, among the rocks and bushes. The badger continued his course, while the fox, after walking for some distance close in his rear, leaped into the water. Scarcely had he disappeared, when on came the pack at full speed, in pursuit. The fox, however, by this time was far away, floating down the stream; but the dogs instantly set upon the luckless badger and tore him to pieces, before they discovered that they had not got Reynard in their clutches.

Evil-doers seldom scruple to let others suffer, so that they may escape. Keep altogether out of the places frequented by such.

THE FOX AND THE BADGER.

THE FOX AND THE HARES.

I HAVE still another story to tell about cunning Reynard. Daylight had just broke, when a well-known naturalist, gun in hand, wandering in search of specimens, observed a large fox making his way along the skirts of a plantation. Reynard looked cautiously over the turf-wall into the neighbouring field, longing evidently to get hold of some of the hares feeding in it, well aware that he had little chance of catching one by dint of running. After examining the different gaps in the wall, he fixed on one which seemed to be the most frequented, and laid himself down close to it, in the attitude of a cat watching a mouse-hole. He next scraped a small hollow in the ground, to form a kind of screen. Now and then he stopped to listen, or take a cautious peep into the field. This done, he again laid himself down, and remained motionless, except when occasionally his eagerness induced him to reconnoitre the feeding hares.

One by one, as the sun rose, they made their way from the field to the plantation. Several passed, but he moved not, except to crouch still closer to the ground. At length two came directly towards him. The involuntary motion of his ears, though he did not venture to look up, showed that he was aware of their approach. Like lightning, as they were leaping through the gap, Reynard was upon them, and catching one, killed her immediately. He was decamping with his booty, when a rifle-ball put an end to his career.

BIRDIE, THE ARCTIC FOX.

I MUST tell you one more story about a fox, and a very interesting little animal it was, though not less cunning than its relatives in warmer regions.

Mr. Hayes, the Arctic explorer, had a beautiful little snow-white fox, which was his companion in his cabin when his vessel was frozen up during the winter. She had been caught in a trap, but soon became tame, and used to sit in his lap during meals, with her delicate paws on the cloth. A plate and fork were provided for her, though she was unable to handle the fork herself; and little bits of raw venison, which she preferred to seasoned food. When she took the morsels into her mouth, her eyes sparkled with delight. She used to wipe her lips, and look up at her master with a *coquetterie* perfectly irresistible. Sometimes she exhibited much impatience; but a gentle rebuke with a fork on the tip of the nose was sufficient to restore her patience.

When sufficiently tame, she was allowed to run loose in the cabin; but she got into the habit of bounding over the shelves, without much regard for the valuable and perishable articles lying on them. She soon also found out the bull's-eye overhead, through the cracks round which she could sniff the cool air. Close beneath it she accordingly took up her abode; and thence she used to crawl down when dinner was on the table, getting into her master's lap, and looking up longingly and lovingly into his face, sometimes putting out her little tongue with impatience, and

barking, if the beginning of the repast was too long delayed.

To prevent her climbing, she was secured by a slight
chain.   This she soon managed to break, and once having
performed the operation, she did not fail to attempt it
again.   To do this, she would first draw herself back as
far as she could get, and then suddenly dart forward, in the
hope of snapping it by the jerk; and though she was thus
sent reeling on the floor, she would again pick herself up,
panting as if her little heart would break, shake out her
disarranged coat, and try once more.   When observed, however, she would sit quietly down, cock her head cunningly
on one side, follow the chain with her eye along its whole
length to its fastening on the floor, walk leisurely to that
point, hesitating a moment, and then make another plunge.
All this time she would eye her master sharply, and if he
moved, she would fall down on the floor at once, and pre-
tend to be asleep.

She was a very neat and cleanly creature, everlastingly
brushing her clothes, and bathing regularly in a bath of
snow provided for her in the cabin.   This last operation
was her great delight.   She would throw up the white
flakes with her diminutive nose, rolling about and burying
herself in them, wipe her face with her soft paws, and then
mount to the side of the tub, looking round her knowingly,
and barking the prettiest bark that ever was heard.   This
was her way of enforcing admiration; and being now satisfied with her performance, she would give a goodly number
of shakes to her sparkling coat, then, happy and refreshed,
crawl into her airy bed in the bull's-eye, and go to sleep.

Mr. Hayes does not tell us what became of Birdie. I am afraid that her fate was a sad one.

THE POLAR BEAR AND HER CUBS.

THE monarch of the Arctic regions, the monstrous white bear there reigns supreme. Savage and ferocious as is his consort, as well as he, she shows the utmost affection for her young. I have a sad tale to tell.

The crew of an exploring vessel in the Arctic Seas had killed a walrus, and set fire to part of the blubber. The steam of the flesh drew from afar towards it a she bear and her two cubs. Putting their noses to the tempting mess, they began to eat it eagerly. The seamen, seeing this, threw other pieces on the ice nearer to the ship. The bear incautiously approached, carrying off the pieces, which she bestowed on her cubs, and, though evidently famished, taking but a small portion herself. The thoughtless sailors shot the two cubs, and again firing, wounded the mother. Though she herself was barely able to crawl to the spot where they lay, she carried to them the last lump of blubber, endeavouring to make them eat it. Discovering that they were unable to do so, she endeavoured to raise first one, and then the other; but in vain. She now began to retreat; but her motherly feelings overcoming her, though conscious of the danger she was running, she returned to where they lay, moaning mournfully. Several times did she thus behave, when, seemingly convinced that her young ones were cold and helpless, she cast a reproachful glance towards the vessel whence the cruel bullets had proceeded, and uttered a low growl of angry despair which might have moved the hearts even of the most callous. A shower of musket bullets, however, laid her low between her two cubs, and she died licking their wounds.

You cry "Shame" on the rough sailors for their cruelty. Yes, they acted cruelly, because they were thoughtless of the feelings of the poor bear. Ask yourself, dear young friend, if you are ever thoughtless of the feelings of those who merit your tenderest love. If you are, cry "Shame" on yourself, and endeavour in future to regard them first of all things.

THE HONEY-SEEKER AND THE BEAR.

THE Indian believes the bear to be possessed not only of a wonderful amount of sagacity, but of feelings akin to those of human beings. Though most species are savage when irritated, some of them occasionally exhibit good-humour and kindness.

A story is told of a man in Russia, who, on an expedition in search of honey, climbed into a high tree. The trunk was hollow, and he discovered a large cone within. He was descending to obtain it, when he stuck fast. Unable to extricate himself, and too far from home to make his voice heard, he remained in that uncomfortable position for two days, sustaining his life by eating the honey. He had become silent from despair, when, looking up, what was his horror to see a huge bear above him, tempted by the same object which had led him into his dangerous

THE POLAR BEAR AND HER CUBS

predicament, and about to descend into the interior of the tree !

Bears—very wisely—when getting into hollows of rocks or trees, go tail-end first, that they may be in a position to move out again when necessary.   No sooner, in spite of his dismay, did the tail of the bear reach him, than the man caught hold of it.   The animal, astonished at finding some big creature below him, when he only expected to meet with a family of bees, against whose stings his thick hide was impervious, quickly scrambled out again, dragging up the man, who probably shouted right lustily.   Be that as it may, the bear waddled off at a quick rate, and the honey-seeker made his way homeward, to relate his adventure, and relieve the anxiety of his family.

THE GOOD-NATURED BEAR AND THE CHILDREN.

THE brown bear, which lives in Siberia, may be considered among the most good-natured of his tribe.   Mr. Atkinson, who travelled in that country, tells us that some peasants— a father and mother—had one day lost two of their children, between four and six years of age.   It was soon evident that their young ones had wandered away to a distance from their home, and as soon as this discovery was made they set off in search of them.

Having proceeded some way through the wilds, they caught sight in the distance of a large animal, which, as they got nearer, they discovered to be a brown bear ; and what was their horror to see within its clutches their lost young ones! Their sensations of dismay were exchanged for astonishment, when they saw the children running about, laughing, round the bear, sometimes taking it by the paws, and sometimes pulling it by the tail. The monster, evidently amused with their behaviour, treated them in the most affectionate manner. One of the children now produced some fruit, with which it fed its shaggy playfellow, while the other climbed up on its back, and sat there, fearlessly urging its strange steed to move on. The parents gave way to cries of terror at seeing the apparent danger to which their offspring were exposed. The little boy, however, having slipped off the bear's back, the animal, hearing the sound of their voices, left the children, and retreated quietly into the forest.

THE WISE HARE AND HER PURSUERS.

I WILL now tell you a story of a very different animal—the timid little hare—which has to depend for safety, not, like the bear, on strength, but on speed and cunning.

A poor little hare was one day closely pursued by a brace of greyhounds, when, seeing a gate near, she ran for it. The bars were too close to allow the hounds to get through, so they had to leap over the gate. As they did so, the hare, perceiving that they would be upon her the next instant, turned round, and ran again under the gate, where she had just before passed. The impetus of the hounds had sent them a considerable distance, and they had now to wheel about and leap once more over the upper bar of the gate. Again she doubled, and returned by the way she had come; and thus, going backwards and forwards, the dogs followed till they were fairly tired out, while the little hare, watching her opportunity, happily made her escape.

You may learn a lesson even from this little hare, never to yield to difficulties. Persevere, and you will surmount them at last.

THE CUNNING WOLF.

Two hundred years ago there were wolves in Ireland, and it appears that they were as cunning as the foxes of the present day.

A man, travelling, as was the custom in those times, on horseback, with a sword by his side, was passing between two towns, some three miles from each other, when he was attacked by a wolf. He drove him off with his sword, but again and again the animal assaulted him. He had nearly reached the town to which he was going, when he met a friend who was unarmed, whom he told of the danger he had encountered; and, as he believed himself now safe from attack, he gave him the sword for his defence. The wolf had been watching this proceeding, evidently intent on attacking the person who was travelling without a sword. When he saw that the first he had attacked was now defenceless, he made after him at full speed, and overtaking him before he got into the town, leaped upon him, unarmed as he now was, and deprived him of life.

When striving for an object, continue your efforts and be cautious, as at the first, till you have gained it.

THE WISE HARE AND HER PURSUERS.

THE TIGER AND THE PARIAH-DOG.

I HAVE told you of a friendship formed between a tiger and a dog. I will now narrate another tale, which speaks well for the good feeling of both animals.

In India it is the cruel custom, when a wandering dog is found, to throw it into a tiger's cage for the purpose of getting rid of it. It happened that one of these pariah-dogs was thrust into the den of the savage beast. The dog, however, instead of giving himself up for lost, stood on the defensive in the corner of the cage, and whenever the tiger approached, seized him by the lip or neck, making him roar piteously. The tiger, savage for want of food, continued to renew the attack, with the same result; till at length the larger animal began to show a respect for the courage of the smaller one, and an understanding was finally arrived at between them.

At last a mess of rice and milk was put into the cage of the tiger, when he invited the dog to partake of it, and instead of treacherously springing on him, as some human beings would have done on their foe, allowed him to feed in quiet. From that day the animals not only became reconciled, but a strong attachment sprang up between them. The dog used to run in and out of the cage, looking upon it as his home; and when the tiger died, he long evidently mourned the loss of his friend and former antagonist.

Observe how that poor outcast dog, by his courage and perseverance, preserved his life, and indeed gained a victory, in spite of the fierce assaults of his savage foe. Will you act less courageously when attacked by the ridicule, the abuse, or the persuasions of those who may try to drag you from the path of duty ?

THE DOE-CHAMOIS AND HER YOUNG.

THE agile inhabitant of the lofty Alps—the graceful chamois—shows the greatest affection for her young.

A Swiss hunter, while pursuing his dangerous sport, observed a mother chamois and her two kids on a rock above him. They were sporting by her side, leaping here and there around her. While she watched their gambols, she was ever on the alert lest an enemy should approach.

The hunter, climbing the rock, drew near, intending, if possible, to capture one of the kids alive. No sooner did the mother chamois observe him, than, dashing at him furiously, she endeavoured to hurl him with her horns down the cliff. The hunter, knowing that he might kill her at any moment, drove her off, fearing to fire, lest the young ones should take to flight.

He was aware that a deep chasm existed beyond them, by which he believed the escape of the animals to be cut off. What was his surprise, therefore, when he saw the old chamois approach the chasm, and, stretching out her fore and hind legs, thus form with her body a bridge across it !

As soon as she had done this, she called on her young ones, and they sprang, one at a time, on her back, and reached the other side in safety ! By a violent effort, she sprang across after them, and soon conducted her charges beyond the reach of the hunter's bullets.

Trust your mother : she, in most cases, will find means
to help you out of trouble.

———

THE CAPTURED WOLF.

I HAVE very little to say in favour of wolves. They are
generally as cowardly in their adversity as they are savage
when at liberty. I give you the following story, however,
which I believe to be true.

An English sportsman had been hunting during the
winter in Hungary. He was returning in a sleigh one
evening to the village where he was to remain for the
night, the peasant owning the sleigh sitting behind, and a
boy driving. As they passed the corner of a wood, a wolf
was seen to rush out of it and give chase. The peasant
shouted to the boy, " A wolf, a wolf ! Drive on, drive on !"
Obeying the order, with whip and shout the boy urged the
horses to full speed. One glance round showed him the
savage animal close behind. The wolf was gaining upon
them fast. The village was scarcely two hundred yards off.
The owner, however, saw that the wolf would be upon them
before they could reach it. Frantically they shouted, pursuing their impetuous career.

Taking another glance behind him, the peasant saw the
fierce, panting beast about to make his fatal spring. A
thought struck him. Seizing the thick sheep-skin which
covered the sleigh, he threw it over his head. Scarcely had
he done so when the wolf sprang upon his back, and griped
hold of the skin. In an instant more it would have been

THE DOE-CHAMOIS AND HER YOUNG.

torn from him, when, raising both his hands, he grasped
the wolf's head and neck with all his strength, hugging
him with an iron clutch to his shoulders. "On—on!" he
shouted to the almost paralyzed driver. The courageous
fellow still holding his fierce assailant in a death-gripe, the
sleigh swept into the village. The inhabitants, hearing
the shouts, rushed forth from their huts, and seeing the
perilous condition of their friends, gave chase with axes in
their hands. No sooner had the boy slackened the speed
of his horses, than the men rushed at the savage animal,
still held captive, and quickly despatched it. Not without
difficulty, however, could the brave peasant, after the
exertion he had undergone, loosen his arms from the neck
of the wolf.

THE TAME OTTER.

THE otter, although not so expert an architect as the beaver,
appears to possess more sagacity. A fine one, caught in
Scotland, became so tame, that whenever it was alarmed it
would spring for protection into the arms of its master.

It had also been taught to fish for his benefit; and so
dexterous was it at this sport, that it would catch several
fine salmon during the day, in a stream near his house. It
could fish as well in salt water as in fresh. Bravely it
would buffet the waves of the ocean, and swim off in chase
of cod-fish, of which it would in a short time catch large
numbers.

When fatigued by its exertions, nothing would induce it
to re-enter the water. On such occasions it received a part of

THE TAME OTTER.

the produce of the sport for its own share ; and after having satisfied itself, it would fall asleep, and was generally in that condition carried home, to resume its labours on another day.

Though you may be very young and small, you may, if you try, help those much older and bigger than yourself.

THE OTTER AND HER YOUNG ONES.

I HAVE another story about an otter, which lived in the Zoological Gardens in London. The otter-pond, surrounded by a wall, was on one occasion only half-full of water, when the otter for whose use it was intended had a pair of young ones. They, happening to fall into the water, were unable to climb up its steep sides. The mother, afraid that they would be drowned, endeavoured in vain, by stooping over the wall, to drag them out. At last she jumped in, and after playing with them for a short time, was seen to put her head to the ear of one of the little creatures. This was to tell her child what she wanted it to do. Directly after, she sprang out of the pond, while her young one caught hold of the fur at the root of her tail ; and while it clung tightly to her, she dragged it out, and placed it safely on the dry ground. She then again plunged in, and in the same way dragged out her other young one.

I am very sure that your parents will help you out of any difficulty into which you may fall; but then you must do as they tell you, thus following the example of the young otters.

THE OTTEH AND HER YOUNG ONES

THE WISE BEAVER.

You have often heard of the wonderful way in which beavers in America construct their habitations and dams. They seem, however, in these operations, to be influenced by instinct rather than by reason. I will tell you of a beaver which lived in captivity in France.

To supply him with nourishment, all sorts of things—fruits, vegetables, and small branches of trees—were thrown to him. His keepers, knowing that he came from a cold climate, bestowed little care, however, in keeping him warm. Winter coming on, one night large flakes of snow were driven by the wind into a corner of his cage. The poor beaver, who, in his own country, forms a remarkably warm house for himself, almost perished with the cold. If man would not help him, he must try and help himself to build a cell which would shelter him from the icy blast. The materials at his disposal were the branches of trees given him to gnaw. These he interwove between the bars of his cage, filling up the interstices with the carrots and apples which had been thrown in for his food. Besides this, he plastered the whole with snow, which froze during the night; and next morning it was found that he had built a wall of considerable height, which perfectly answered his purpose.

Make the best of the means at your disposal, as well as of the talents you possess.

THE RAT AND THE SWAN.

RATS, in their ferocity, partake of the character of the wolf, and in their cunning, of that of the fox.

A great flood occurred some years ago in the north of England ; and as a number of people were collected on the banks of the Tyne, whose waters had risen to an unusual height, a swan was seen swimming across the flood. On its back was a black spot, visible among its white plumage. As the swan came nearer, this was found to be a live rat. No sooner had the swan, after bravely breasting the foaming torrent, reached the shore, than the rat leaped off and scampered away. Probably it had been carried into the water, and, unable to swim to land, on seeing the swan had sought refuge on its back, thus escaping a watery grave.

As the swan did, help those incapable of helping themselves, though you dislike their appearance and character. They may not have had the advantages you possess.

THE RATS AND THE WINE-CASK.

AN old lady, wealthy and hospitable, lived in a large house, with several servants to attend on her. Although no terrific murder or other dark deed was ever known to have been perpetrated in the house, report said it was haunted. Undoubtedly, noises were heard in the lower part of the mansion. Night after night unearthly sounds arose after the domestics had retired to their chambers. At last the old lady, determined to resist this invasion of her domestic peace, told her servants to arm themselves with such weapons as they could obtain, she herself sitting up with a brace of loaded pistols before her. This proceeding had the desired effect. The ghostly visitants, if such they were, ceased from their nocturnal revels. All remained silent till cock-crow. Night after night the brave old dame heroically watched, but no ghosts came.

To celebrate her victory, she invited a number of guests, and determined to broach a cask of long-hoarded Madeira. With keys in hand, attended by the butler, she entered the cellar; the spill was pulled out from the cask, the cock duly inserted, but no wine came. The butler tapped; a hollow sound was the return. On applying a light, teeth-marks were visible at the very lowest part of the staves.

By rats alone could such marks have been made. What a band of thirsty topers must have been employed in the nefarious burglary! No doubt it was the rats, inebriated by such unusual potations, which had caused the mysterious uproar. Be that as it may, the lady lost her wine; and the cask was placed in the museum of Mr. Buckland, who tells the tale, and there it stands to corroborate its truth.

It is said that rats will insert their tails into oil-flasks, and allow each other in turn to suck off the liquid thus obtained.

THE MOUSE AND THE HONEY-POT.

MICE, I suspect, are fully as sagacious as rats; perhaps they are more so. In their foraging expeditions what cleverness

THE RATS AND THE WINE-CASK.

do they exhibit !   When one or two have been caught in a trap, how careful are the rest of the community not to be tempted by the treacherous bait.

A honey-pot had been left in a closet, from the wall of which some of the loose plaster had fallen down.   In the morning, the honey being wanted, the pot was found with a considerable portion abstracted.   Outside of it was a heap of mortar reaching to the edge, forming an inclined plane, while inside a similar structure had been raised with the loose plaster.   From the marks on the shelf, it was clearly the work of a mouse ; which had thus, by means of a well-designed structure, obtained entrance and exit.

If a little mouse, to gain its object, which you deem a wrong one, can employ so much intelligence, how much more should you exert your superior faculties to attain a right object.

THE EWE WHICH RETURNED TO HER OLD HOME.

I HAVE told you of dogs making their way from one end of the country to the other in search of their masters, and of horses traversing wide districts to the pastures where they were bred, but you would scarcely expect to hear of a sheep performing a long journey to return to the home of her youth.

A ewe, bred in the neighbourhood of Edinburgh, was driven into Perthshire, a distance of upwards of one hundred miles.   She remained some time at the place, and there became the mother of a lamb.   She took a dislike to her new home, and thoughts of her early days stealing

THE EWE WHICH RETURNED TO HER OLD HOME.

upon her, she came to the resolution of returning to the scenes of her youth.

Calling her lamb, she one night set off southward.   Often she was compelled to hurry on her young one with impatient bleatings.   She took the highroad, along which she had been driven.   Reaching Stirling early in the morning, she discovered that an annual fair was taking place, and that the town was full of people.   Unwilling to venture among them for fear of being caught, or losing her lamb, she waited patiently outside till the evening, lying close by the road-side.   Many people saw her, but believing her owner was near, did not molest her.   During the early hours of the morning she got safely through, observed by several people, and evidently afraid lest the dogs prowling about the town might injure her young one.

Arriving at length at the toll-bar of St. Ninians, she was stopped by the toll-keeper, who supposed her to be a stray sheep.   She escaped him, however, and several times when the gate was opened endeavoured, with the lamb at her heels, to make her way through.   He each time drove her back.   She at length turned round, and appeared to be going the way she came.   She had, however, not abandoned her intention, for she either discovered a more circuitous road to the south side of the gate, or made her way through; for on a Sabbath morning early in June she arrived at the farm where she had been bred,—having been nine days on her journey.

So delighted was her former owner with this exhibition of affection for the farm, and with her wonderful memory, that he offered her purchaser the price he had received;

and to the day of her death—when she had reached the mature age, for a sheep, of seventeen years—she remained a constant resident on her native farm.

THE EWE AND HER LAMB.

THERE is another story about a ewe which I should like to tell you, and which shows the affection she had for her young.

A lamb, frisking about near its mother, contrived to spring into a thick hedge, in which its coat was so firmly held that it could not escape. The ewe, after vainly trying to rescue her young one, ran off with violent bleatings towards a neighbouring field, breaking in her way through several hedges, to where there was a ram, and communicated to him the disaster. He at once returned with her, and by means of his horns quickly pushed the young creature out of the thorny entanglement in which it had been entrapped.

o

THE TWO WISE GOATS.

ON the crumbling walls of the romantic ruins of Caernarvon Castle, some years ago, two agile goats were seen,—now leaping over a rugged gap, now climbing some lofty pinnacle, now browsing on the herbage overhanging the perilous paths. Presently they approached each other from opposite ends of one of the narrow intersecting walls. When they met, finding that there was no room to pass, they surveyed each other face to face for some minutes in perfect stillness.   Each had barely standing ground for his own feet.   However, they tossed their heads with menacing looks, often making slight feints of butting or pushing forward ; but they took care not to come into actual contact, knowing well that the slightest force might precipitate one or both from their perilous position.   Neither could they attempt to walk backward or turn round on so narrow a spot.   Thus they again stood quite still for above an hour, occasionally uttering low sounds, but neither of them moving.

At length they appeared to have settled the difficult point as to which of the two should give way.   The one which appeared the youngest lay quietly down, while the other walked calmly over him, and pursued his path contentedly.

Their example might well be followed by human beings in many of the affairs of life, where a contest must prove destructive to both.   Many a bloody war might be averted, did nations imitate the example of these two animals.   Not, however, by bowing the neck to the yoke of a conqueror, but by amicably settling differences.   How many law-suits might also be avoided by the same means.

And you, my young friends, understand that there is far more true magnanimity and courage exhibited in giving way to others than in battling for doubtful rights and privileges.

THE AFFECTIONATE SEAL.

IF you have ever examined the head of a seal, with its large gentle eyes, you will readily believe that the animal

THE AFFECTIONATE SEAL.

possesses a certain amount of intellect, and is capable of very affectionate feelings.

The story I am about to tell you is a very sad one. Perhaps you will recollect the seal in the Zoological Gardens, which used to come out of its pond at the call of the French sailor to whom it belonged, and, climbing up while he sat on a chair, put its fins round his neck and give him a kiss. How it immediately obeyed him when he told it to go back to the water, and how adroitly it used to catch the fish which he threw to it. I remember also hearing of a seal in Shetland which would return with its prey in its mouth on being summoned by the owner.

But the seal I am going to tell you about belonged to a gentleman in the west of Ireland, near the sea. This seal was so tame, and so attached to its master, that it would follow him about like a dog, and seemed much pleased whenever allowed to lick his hand.

People in that part of the country are sadly ignorant and superstitious. Two bad harvests having succeeded each other, the foolish inhabitants took it into their heads that the disaster was caused by the innocent seal. So many were the complaints they made, some people even threatening the owner, that, fearing the life of his favourite would be endangered, he was obliged to consent to its being sent away. Having been put on board a boat, it was taken to some distance and then thrown into the sea. Very shortly afterwards, however, it found its way back to its beloved master. Still anxious to preserve the animal's life, he consented to its being again carried away to a greater distance;

but once more it returned. This made the ignorant people more certain than ever that the poor seal was some evil being.

Again it was put on board a boat, the crew of which rowed to a much greater distance than before, determining that the poor seal should trouble them no more. Though following the injunctions of their master not to kill it, they cruelly put out its eyes, and then threw it overboard, to perish in the wide ocean, as they believed. Some time passed, when one stormy night the gentleman heard above the moaning sounds of the gale the plaintive cry of his favourite close to his house. He went to the door, and, opening it, there lay the body of the affectionate animal quite dead. Though deprived of its sight, it had found its way back to the shore on which its master's house stood, and exerting all its strength, had crawled up to the door; thus exhibiting an amount of affection for its human friend such as can scarcely exist in a greater degree in the breast of any animal.

CHAPTER VIII.

Birds.

WHEN we observe the small heads and unmeaning eyes of birds, we do not expect to find any great amount of intellect among them. They are, however, moved by the same passions and feelings as larger animals, and occasionally exhibit thought and reasoning power. I suspect, indeed, could we understand their language, that we should find they can talk to each other, and express their meaning as well as others of the brute creation.

THE GANDER AND THE BANTAM-COCK.

A GOOSE was seated on her eggs in a quiet corner, not far from a horse-pond, in a farmyard. Up and down before her strode a game-cock, which, watching the calm looks and contented manner of the goose, which contrasted so greatly with his own fiery disposition, began to get angry,—just as human beings who are out of sorts sometimes do with

THE GANDER AND THE BANTAM-COCK.

those who appear happy and smiling. At last, working himself into a downright passion, he flew at the poor goose, pecked out one of her eyes, and while she was attempting to defend herself, trampled on and destroyed several of her eggs. The gander, which was waddling about on the other side of the pond, on seeing what was taking place hastened to the aid of his consort, and attacked the savage cock. The cock of course turned upon him, and a desperate battle ensued. The two combatants, after a time, drew off from each other, both probably claiming the victory.

For some days after this, the cock, taught prudence, allowed the goose to remain in quiet, the gander watching him narrowly. The latter at last, trusting to the lesson he had given the cock, wandered away for provender to a distant part of the yard. No sooner was he gone than the cock, which had all the time been waiting for an opportunity, again assaulted the poor goose. Her loud cries were fortunately heard by the gander, which came tearing along with outstretched wings to her assistance, and seizing the cock by the neck, before the angry bird could turn his head, he hauled him along to the pond. In he plunged, and soon had him in deep water. "I am more than your master now," thought the gander, as he ducked the cock under the surface; "I will take care you shall never more interfere with my dear goose." And again and again he ducked the cock, keeping his head each time longer under water, till at last his struggles ceased, and he was drowned.

It is sinful to harbour the slightest feeling of revenge in our hearts; yet those who attack others unable to defend themselves, either by word or deed, must expect to receive deserved punishment from the more powerful friends of their victims.

~~~~~~~~~~

THE FARMER AND HIS GOOSE.

A CHESHIRE farmer had a large flock of geese. As he was passing through the yard one day, one of the geese quitted its companions and stalked after him. Why it did so he could never tell, as he had shown it no more attention than the rest of the flock. The following day the goose behaved in the same way; and at length, wherever he went—to the mill, the blacksmith's shop, or even through the bustling streets of the neighbouring town—the goose followed at his heels. When he went to church, he was obliged to shut up the goose.

While ploughing his fields, the goose would walk sedately before him, with firm step, and head and neck erect—frequently turning round and fixing its eyes upon him. One furrow completed, and the plough turned, the goose, without losing step, would adroitly wheel about; and would thus behave, till it followed its master home.

Even in the house, as he sat by the fire in the evening, it would mount on his lap, nestle its head in his bosom, and preen his hair with its beak, as it was wont to do its own feathers.

Even when he went out shooting, the goose followed like a dog, getting over the fences as well as he could himself.

It is sad to think that gross superstition was the cause of the death of the faithful bird. The ignorant farmer afterwards killed it, fancying that the mysterious affection of the goose boded him some evil.

Take warning from the fate of the poor goose, and do not bestow your affection on those who seem unworthy of it, however clever or powerful they may be.

THE BLIND WOMAN AND HER GANDER.

BISHOP STANLEY, who mentions the story, heard of an aged blind woman who used to be led every Sunday to church by a gander, which took hold of her gown with its bill. When she had seated herself, it retired to graze in the churchyard till she came out again, and then it would lead her safely home.

One day the clergyman called at her house, and expressed his surprise to the daughter that the mother should venture abroad. She replied : "O sir, we are not afraid of trusting her out of sight, for the gander is with her."

When a poor despised goose can thus make itself of so much use, how much more should you try to become useful.

THE PRISONER SET FREE.

MRS. F——, who has had much experience with poultry, considers them very sensible and kind-hearted birds. The leg of a young duck had been broken by an accident. She placed it in splints, and put the bird under a small crate, on a patch of grass, to prevent its moving about till it had recovered. It was one of a large family; and in a short time its relatives gathered round the prisoner, clamouring their condolence in every variety of quacking intonation. They forced their necks under the crate, evidently trying to raise it, and thus liberate the captive; but the effort was beyond their strength. Convinced, at length, of this, after clamouring a little more they marched away in a body, while the prisoner quietly sat down and appeared resigned.

A short time afterwards a great deal of quacking was heard, and a regiment of upwards of forty ducks was seen marching into the yard, headed by two handsome drakes, known by the names of Robin Hood and Friar Tuck. Evidently with a preconceived purpose, they all marched up to the crate and surrounded it. Every neck was thrust beneath the lowest bar of the prison; every effort was made to raise it,—but in vain. At length a parley ensued. Then the noise ceased. Only the deep-toned quacking of Robin Hood was heard, when their object became clear. All the tribe gathered together on one side of the crate, the strongest in front; and as many as could reach it thrust their necks beneath the crate, while the rest pushed them forward from behind. Thus they succeeded in overturning the crate, and setting free their imprisoned friend. With clamorous rejoicings from the whole troop, the liberated duck limped off in their midst.

These sensible ducks teach us the important lesson that union is strength. Not that they, you will agree with me, showed their wisdom exactly in liberating their companion, who was placed in confinement for his benefit. However, remember through life how much you may effect in a good cause by sinking all minor differences, and uniting with others like-minded with yourself.

THE TWO SPORTING FRIENDS.

MY children have a black dog and a jackdaw; and though the bird shows a preference for human companionship, when he cannot obtain that he hops off to the dog's kennel, on the top of which he sits, talking to his four-footed friend in his own fashion; and the dog seems well-pleased to receive his visits. I fully expect, some day, to have some curious tale to tell about them.

In the meantime, I will tell you of a raven which had been brought up with a dog in Cambridgeshire. They had formed an alliance, offensive and defensive, and could certainly interchange ideas. The dog was fond of hares and rabbits, and the raven had no objection to a piece of game for his dinner. Being both at liberty, they used to set out together into the country to hunt. The dog would enter a cover and drive out the hares or rabbits, when the raven, which was watching outside, would pounce down on the animals as they rushed from the thicket, and hold them till the dog came to its assistance. They thus managed to obtain their desired feast—indeed, they were probably more successful than many human sportsmen.

THE TWO SPORTING FRIENDS.

THE TWO HENS.

IN Mrs. F——'s poultry-yard, some duck-eggs had been placed under a Dorking hen. A few days afterwards, a bantam began to sit on her own eggs—the nests being close together. In the accustomed twenty-one days the bantams were hatched and removed; but after the usual thirty days required for hatching the duck-eggs had passed, none appeared, and so the Dorking hen was taken away and the nest destroyed. Although ten days had elapsed since the hatching of the bantam's eggs, the Dorking hen remembered her neighbour's good fortune, and tried to get possession of her brood—calling the little ones, feeding them, and fighting to keep them; but the true mother would by no means consent to resign her rights. To prevent the interference of the Dorking, she was shut up for several days; but directly she was liberated, she again flew to the little chickens and acted as before.

Two Muscovy ducklings having just been hatched under another hen, they were offered, as a consolation for her disappointment, to the Dorking; and such was her desire for maternity that she instantly adopted them. To prevent further trouble, she and her charges were sent to a neighbouring house. A fortnight later other ducks were hatched, and as it seemed a pity to waste the time of the banished hen with two ducklings only, they were sent for home. The little Muscovies were placed with their own brethren, and the hen turned loose among the rest of the poultry, it being supposed impossible that she would still recollect the past. Her memory, however, was more tenacious than any one fancied. Once more she hastened to the bantams, and lavished her care on the tiny things, of whom only three were surviving. The bantam mother, on this, appeared satisfied to regard her as a friend. They disputed no longer, but jointly and equally lavished their cares and caresses on the three chicks.

Here is not only a curious example of tenacity of memory, but it is the only instance of friendship Mrs. F—— has ever known to exist amongst gallinaceous fowl.

Do not be jealous of another's success, but try rather to assist and support a rival, if your services are acceptable.

THE WILD TURKEY AND THE DOG.

AUDUBON, the American naturalist, whose statements we can thoroughly trust, once possessed a fine male turkey of the wild breed common in the Western States. He had reared the bird till it became so tame that it would follow any one who called it. He had also a favourite spaniel, which became thoroughly intimate with the turkey, and the two might constantly have been seen running side by side. When the bird was about two years old, it would fly into the forest, and occasionally remain away for several days together.

It happened one day, after it had been absent for some time, that as Audubon was walking through the forest at some distance from his home, he saw a turkey get up before him, but he did not recognize it as his own. Wishing to secure it for the table, he ordered his dog to make chase.

Off went the spaniel at full speed ; but the bird, instead of flying away, remained quietly on the ground till its pursuer came up. The dog was then about to seize it, when Audubon saw the former suddenly stop, and turn her head towards him. On hastening up, he discovered, greatly to his surprise, that the turkey was his own. Recognizing the spaniel, it had not flown away from her, as it would have done from a strange dog.

Unhappily, the turkey, again leaving home to range through the forest, was mistaken for a wild one, and accidentally shot. Audubon recognized it by a red ribbon being brought him which he had placed round its neck.

Do not forget old friends or former worthy companions, however humble, but treat them with kindness and consideration.

THE BRAVE HEN.

A SPANISH hen, in Mrs. F——'s poultry-yard, was sitting on her nest in the hatching-house, which had a small window, through which a person might look to see that all was right. As the hens were usually fed upon their nests, the ground was strewed with corn, which tempted the rats and mice. The hens used frequently to punish the mice by a sharp tap on the head with their beak, which laid them to rest for ever.

One day Mrs. F—— was looking through the window, when she saw a middle-sized rat peering forth from its hole. The rat scrambled into the upper range of boxes, where sat the Spanish hen, and then remained awhile still

THE WILD TURKEY AND THE DOG.

as a mouse. The hen evidently saw him, but she sat close, her head drawn back and kept low on the shoulder, her eyes nearly closed. She clearly feigned to be asleep. The rat, deceived, advanced a few steps, and then sat on his haunches, looking and listening with all his might. Again he moved, again paused, then sprang into one corner of the nest, grappling an egg with his fore-paws at the same instant. The hen had never stirred all the time; but now, suddenly throwing forward her head, she seized her foe by the nape of the neck; then, without withdrawing her bill, she pressed down his head repeatedly with all her force. She then gave an extra peck or two, half rose, settled her eggs beneath her again, and seemed happy; and before her lay a half-grown rat, quite dead.

This was, indeed, calm courage. Imitate, if you can, this brave hen. Endeavour to be cool and collected when danger approaches.

THE GALLANT SWAN AND HIS FOE.

SWANS show much bravery, especially in defending their young; indeed, from their size, they are able to do battle with the largest of the feathered tribe. They have been known also to attack people who have ventured nearer their cygnets than they liked.

I remember a lady being attacked by a swan on the banks of a lake, in the grounds of a relative of mine. She had to take to flight, and was met running along the path crying for aid, with the swan, its wings outstretched, in full chase after her.

THE GALLANT SWAN AND HIS FOE.

Only lately, a person paddling in a canoe near Chelmsford approached a nest of cygnets, when the parent swan swam out, and seizing the bow of the canoe, nearly upset it. The paddler had to back out of the way, with difficulty escaping the violent assaults of the enraged bird.

One morning, as a family of cygnets were assembled on the banks of one of the islands in the Zoological Gardens of London, and the parent birds were swimming about watching their little ones, a carrion-crow, thinking that the old birds were too far off to interfere with him, pounced down on one of the cygnets. The father swan, however, had his eye on the marauder, and, darting forward, seized him with his bill. The crow in vain struggled to get free. The swan, like the gander I before mentioned, dragged the felon towards the lake, and plunging him under water, held him there till his caws sounded no longer.

Be brave and bold in defence of the helpless, especially of those committed to your charge.

THE RAVEN AND THE BIRD-TRAP.

RAVENS are supposed to be the most cunning and sagacious of birds. They are knowing fellows, at all events.

Some school-boys in Ireland used frequently to set traps for catching birds. A tame raven belonging to their family frequently watched the proceedings of the young gentlemen, and it occurred to him that he had as much right to the birds as they had. When, therefore, they were out of the way, he would fly down to the trap and lift the lid ; but as he could not hold it up and seize his prey at the same time, the bird invariably escaped.

Not far off lived another tame raven, with which he was on visiting acquaintance. After having vainly attempted on frequent occasions to get the birds out of the trap by himself, he one day observed another poor bird caught. Instead, however, of running the risk of opening the trap as before, he hastened off to his acquaintance. The two ravens then came back to the trap, and while one lifted the lid, the other seized the poor captive. They then divided their prize between them.

When you see rogues like these two ravens agree, do you not feel ashamed when you take so little pains to assist your companions in doing what is right ? We are placed in this world to help one another.

THE FACETIOUS RAVEN.

A LARGE dog was kept chained in a stable-yard, in the roof of one of the out-buildings of which a raven had his abode. The dog and bird had become great friends. Yet the latter could not help amusing himself at the expense of his four-footed companion. Sometimes he would snatch a piece of food from the dog's pan, often when he did not wish to eat it himself. As the dog submitted without complaint at first, the raven would come again and take another piece away, then bring it back just within reach, and dangle it over the dog's nose. As soon as he opened his mouth to catch it, the raven would dart off again out of his reach.

At other times he would hide a piece just beyond the length of the dog's chain, and then, with a cunning look, perch upon his head.

Yet, mischievous as he was, the bird would never altogether run away with the quadruped's food, but would after a while return it, with the exception of any small bit which he might wish to keep for himself. These tricks in no way offended the good-natured dog. He showed a remarkable instance of his affection, when on one occasion the raven happened to tumble into a tub of water, just beyond his range. Seeing the poor bird struggling, he exerted all his strength, and dragged his heavy kennel forward till he could put his head over the edge of the tub, when he took the raven up in his mouth and laid him gently on the ground to recover.

THE ARCTIC RAVEN.

RAVENS vie with our brave Arctic explorers in the wide circuit they make in their wanderings.

When Captain M'Clure was frozen up in the ice, during his last expedition to the North Pole, two ravens settled themselves near his ship, for the sake of obtaining the scraps of food thrown to them by the seamen. A dog belonging to the ship, however, regarding their pickings as an encroachment on his rights, used, as they drew near, to rush forward and endeavour to seize them with his mouth; but the ravens were too cunning to be entrapped in that manner. No sooner were the mess-tins cleared out than they would approach, and as he sprang after them, would fly a few yards off, and there keep a sharp eye on his movements. Having enticed him to a distance, they would fly rapidly towards the ship, with a chuckle of satisfaction ; and before the dog arrived, all the best bits had been secured by his cunning rivals.

THE EAGLE'S NEST.

MAGNIFICENT as the eagle is in appearance, he certainly does not, on the score of intellect, deserve the rank he holds as king of birds. Except that he will fight bravely now and then for his young, I know of no good quality he possesses.

A countryman in the Highlands, to whose farmyard an eagle had paid several unwelcome visits, carrying off ducklings and chickens, determined to have his revenge. Sallying forth, gun in hand, he climbed up the rocky side of a neighbouring mountain, when he saw, high above him, the nest of the eagle. Shouting loudly, he discovered that neither of the parents were at home. Taking off his shoes, he was ascending towards the nest, when, about half-way up, while he was standing on a ledge, holding on tightly to a rock, he espied a hen eagle rapidly approaching, with a supply of food in her beak. Immediately, and with a terrible scream, she darted towards the intruder. Unable to defend himself, he expected to have his eyes torn out, when he let go, and slipped to a broader ledge. Again the eagle pounced upon him ; and so close was she, that even then he could not get a shot at her. In desperation, he took off his bonnet and threw it at the bird. She, seeing it fall, immediately followed it to the foot of the rock. This gave him an opportunity of bringing his gun to bear on her. The shot took effect, and she fell dead far below him.

THE TAME ROBINS.

WHAT interesting, confiding little birds are the robin redbreasts of our own dear England!

It was summer-time. An old lady lay in bed suffering from her last illness. The bed was of large size, with a roof and four posts, the foot of it being not far from the window. The lattice, with its diamond panes, was open from morn till eve; and as the old lady thus lay calm and composed, and often alone, she observed a pair of robins enter by the window and fly round the corner of the roof of her bed. Chirruping to each other, they seemed to agree that just inside of the bed would be a nice spot for building their nest. Away they flew, and soon returned with straws and little sticks. Thus they quickly had a cozy little nest constructed in a secure position, which no bird of prey or marauding cat was likely to reach.

The lady would on no account allow of their being disturbed, and they had free ingress and egress. Here the hen laid her eggs, sitting upon them, while Cock Robin brought her her daily meals. The eggs were hatched, and in this happy abode, greatly to the pleasure of the old lady, their little family was reared; and before she died, they were fully fledged, and had flown away.

THE EAGLE'S NEST

THE AFFECTIONATE DUCK.

A DUCK and drake lived together, as husband and wife should do, in the bonds of mutual affection. The poultry-yard being assailed, the drake was carried off by thieves. The poor bereaved duck exhibited evident signs of grief at her loss. Retiring into a corner, she sat disconsolate all day. No longer did she preen herself, as had been her wont. Scarcely could she be induced to waddle to the pond, nor would she touch the food brought to her. It was thought, indeed, that she would die.

While in this unhappy condition, a drake, which by the same marauders had been deprived of his mate, cast his eyes on her, and began to consider that she might replace his lost companion. She, however, instead of offering him encouragement, repelled his advances with evident disdain.

Search had been made for the thieves; and though they escaped, their booty was discovered, most of the birds alive and well, and among them the affectionate duck's lost husband. On his return to the farmyard, the loving couple exhibited the liveliest joy at meeting. She had a long story to tell, which the drake listened to with stern attention. No sooner was it finished than he glanced fiercely round the farmyard, and then, evidently with fell intentions, made his way towards where the rival drake was digging worms from the soft mud. His pace quickened as he approached his antagonist; then, with a loud quack, he flew at him, brought him to the ground, pecked out first one eye and then the other, and otherwise assaulted him so furiously,

THE AFFECTIONATE DUCK.

that his unfortunate foe sank at length lifeless beneath the blows of his strong bill.

While I describe the bad example set by the drake, I must entreat you not to harbour even for a moment any angry feelings which may arise at injuries done you.

OLD PHIL THE SEA-GULL.

FROM the lofty cliffs at the back of the Isle of Wight, numerous wild-fowl may be seen whirling in rapid flight through the air, now rising above the green downs, now descending to the blue surface of the water. Towards the west end of that romantic island, in a hollow between the cliffs, is the village of Calbourne. Here, some time since, might have been seen, sailing over the village green, Old Phil, one of the white-winged birds I have described. Abandoning the wild freedom of his brethren, he had associated himself with the human inhabitants of the place. His chief friend was a grocer, near whose shop he would alight on a neighbouring wall, and receive with gratitude the bits of cheese and other dainties which were offered him.

At certain times of the year, however, he would take his departure, and generally return with a wife, whom he used to introduce to his old friends, that she might partake of their hospitality. Not, indeed, that she would venture so close to the grocer's shop, even for the sake of the cheese-parings ; but she used to enter the village, and frequently spent her time at a pond hard by, while Old Phil went to pay his respects to the purveyor of groceries.

THE TAME CROW.

IT is interesting to rear up animals or birds, and to watch their progress as they gain strength and sense, and thus remark their various habits and dispositions. Almost invariably, when kindly treated, they return the care spent on them by marks of affection, though some exhibit it in a much less degree than others.

Crows are considered wise birds ; but, while understanding how to take care of themselves, they are not celebrated for their affectionate disposition. Still a crow may become fond of its owner.

A gentleman had reared one from the nest, and it had long dwelt with him, coming at his call, and feeding from his hand. At length it disappeared, and he supposed it to have been killed. About a year afterwards, as he was out walking one day, he observed several crows flying overhead ; when what was his surprise to see one of them leave the flock, fly towards him, and perch on his shoulder ! He at once recognized his old friend, and spoke to it as he had been in the habit of doing. The crow cawed in return, but kept carefully beyond reach of his hand ; showing that, having enjoyed a free existence, it did not intend to submit again to captivity. A few more caws were uttered. Its companions cawed likewise. The crow understood their call. Probably its mate, and perhaps its young ones, were among them. Glancing towards them, and with a farewell caw at its old master, it spread its wings and joined the flock ; nor did it ever again return to its former abode.

You will find it far more easy to give up good habits than to get rid of bad ones. Be careful therefore to cherish the good ones. You can never have too many of them.

THE OSTRICH AND HER YOUNG.

THE ostrich, which, with its long strides and small wings, traverses the sandy deserts of Africa at a rapid rate, lifting its head on the look-out for danger, is generally spoken of as a stupid bird. Notwithstanding this character, it displays great affection for its young, and some sense in other matters. Sometimes a pair may be seen with a troop of twelve or more young ones, watching all their movements, and ready to call them away should a foe appear. Sometimes the young are not much larger than Guinea-fowls; and as their parents are aware that the little birds cannot run so fast as they themselves can, they endeavour, when an enemy comes near, to draw him away from their charges. The female generally undertakes this office, while the cock bird leads the brood in an opposite direction. Now the hen ostrich flies off before the horseman, spreading out or drooping her wings. Now she will throw herself on the ground before the foe, as if wounded, again to rise when he gets too near; and then, wheeling about, she tries to induce him to follow her. Thus she will proceed, trying similar devices, till she fancies that she has led her pursuer to a safe distance from the brood, when, abandoning her former tactics, she will dash off across the plain, fleet as the wind.

THE TAME CROW

THE BLACKBIRDS AND GRIMALKIN.

Two blackbirds had built their nest in the thick bough of a tree which overhung a high paling. Here they fancied themselves secure from the prying eyes of idle boys or marauding cats. The hen laid her eggs in her new abode, and in due time several fledgelings were hatched, which her faithful mate assisted her to rear. While in the full enjoyment of their happiness, watching over their helpless young ones, they one day saw what to them appeared a terrific monster—a large cat—leap to the top of the paling, and begin cautiously creeping along it. So narrow was it, however, that even Grimalkin could not venture to move fast.

The parent blackbirds watched him with beating hearts as he crept on and on, his savage eyes turned up ever and anon when he stepped towards their nest, where their young ones were chirping merrily, unconscious of danger. In another instant he might make his fatal spring, and seize them in his cruel jaws. The heart of the tender mother urged her to risk her own life for the sake of her offspring. Downward she flew, uttering loud screams of anger almost within reach of the marauder, but the narrowness of the paling prevented him from leaping forward and seizing her in his claws. The brave father was not behind his mate in courage. He too pitched on the top of the fence directly in front of Grimalkin. As the cat crept on he retreated, hoping to draw her past his nest; but the cruel plunderer's eye was too securely fixed on that. The cock, seeing this,

THE OSTRICH AND HER YOUNG

darted with the courage of despair on the back of his enemy, and assailed him with such fierce and repeated pecks on the head, that the cat, losing his balance, fell to the ground, and, astonished at the unexpected attack, scampered off, resolved, I hope, **never again** to molest the heroic blackbirds; while they flew back to the nest they had so bravely defended.

CONCLUSION.

I HAVE often thought, while writing these stories, of a remark made by one of my boys, whom, when he was a very little fellow, I took to hear a sermon to children at the Abbey Church of Malvern. The vicar gave a number of interesting anecdotes of children who had assisted poor people, saved up their money for charitable purposes, made collections for missionary objects; who had died young, happy to go to a better world, or had been brought to love Jesus at an early age, and had been the means of inducing their companions to love him too.

My little boy, who was seated in my lap, listened, with eyes fixed on the preacher, to every word that was said. At last one or two accounts were given which seemed to puzzle him greatly, and, casting an inquiring glance into my face, he whispered,—"Papa, papa! is 'um all true?"

Now, perhaps some of you, my young friends, as you read the stories I have given you, will be inclined to ask, as did my little boy, "Is 'um all true?" I can reply to you, as I did to him, "Oh yes; I believe so."

They are generally thoroughly well authenticated. A

THE BLACKBIRDS AND GRIMALKIN

considerable number have been narrated to me by friends who witnessed the behaviour of the animals, while several have come under my own observation.

I trust, therefore, my dear young friends, that the narratives I have given you may not only prove interesting, but that you will learn from them to pay due respect to all animals, however mean and insignificant you have been accustomed to think them. They think and reason in their way. They not only suffer bodily pain, but they have feelings in a remarkable degree like your own; and you must own that it is cruel to hurt those feelings by ill-treatment or neglect.

It is pleasant to read an interesting book; it is good to remember what you read, and better still to gain some useful lessons from it. This, I hope, you will do from these stories about animals and the teachings they afford. I trust, therefore, that you will derive benefit, as well as amusement, from this little book; and with earnest wishes that you may do so, I bid you farewell.

www.ingramcontent.com/pod-product-compliance
Lightning Source LLC
Chambersburg PA
CBHW031406020726
47499CB00005B/1488